Roxy

Roxy

PJ reece

VANCOUVER LONDON

Distribution and representation in the UK by
Turnaround • www.turnaround-uk.com

Published simultaneously in Canada and the UK in 2009
Released in the US in 2010

Mixed Sources
Cert no. SW-COC-001271
© 1996 FSC
FSC
Inside pages printed on FSC certified paper
using vegetable-based inks.

Manufactured by Sunrise Printing
Manufactured in Chilliwack, BC, Canada in October 2009

10 9 8 7 6 5 4 3 2 1

Cataloguing-in-Publication Data for this book
is available from The British Library.

Library and Archives Canada Cataloguing in Publication

Reece, PJ, 1945-
    Roxy / PJ Reece.

ISBN 978-1-896580-01-2

    I. Title.

PS8585.E3477R69 2009   jC813'.54   C2009-904842-6

For Rowan

The publisher wishes to thank Rachel McBrearty and Caroline McLean
for their editorial assistance on this project.

The map on the front cover was first published in The Cyclopaedia:
Universal Dictionary of Arts, Sciences, and Literature *by Abraham Rees (1820)*
and is part of the Map Collection of The Perry-Castañeda Library
at the University of Texas, Austin.

The publisher acknowledges the support of the Canada Council for the Arts.

Canada Council   Conseil des Arts
for the Arts   du Canada

The publisher also wishes to thank the Government of British Columbia for the
financial support it has extended through the book publishing tax credit program
and the British Columbia Arts Council.

BRITISH COLUMBIA
ARTS COUNCIL
Supported by the Province of British Columbia

The publisher also acknowledges the financial support of the Government of
Canada through the Book Publishing Industry Development Program (BPIDP)
and the Association for the Export of Canadian Books (AECB) for our publishing
activities.

Contents

The Myth

Before the phone call, I wasn't quite sure what a myth was. Greek gods were myths; I knew that. And Shangri-La, a paradise hidden somewhere at the top of the world. My grandmother was born there. But she died when she was a teenager, giving birth to my mom. That's where myth stops and the ugly facts begin. My grandfather took one look at that squalling motherless child and fled. How hideous is that?

That's our family history in a rotten little nutshell, infecting our lives like a curse. Just ask my mother, forsaken by her father and then her husband. What made me think my life wouldn't be next to go down the toilet?

Then came the phone call.

That's all I've written on account of this bus. Bumpy! And the road, not exactly a ribbon of moonlight, but I love the way it winds and climbs and clings to the side of the valley. But rough!

"Yii! The road! Where did it go?"

With my forehead pressed against the window, all I see is the bottom of a rocky valley a long way down. And a river, icy blue, like a certain someone's eyes, reminding me why I'm here. I swear to God this bus is going to career over the cliff, and I regret not having finished writing my story. I see rescue workers picking through the smoking wreckage to uncover a charred notebook that contains only those mysterious lines about a myth and a phone call. But nothing about the horrible secret that robbed a girl of her entire life, and not a word about how she got her life back. That phone call did it, triggered an avalanche of events. *Oops*—I retract *avalanche*. They obviously happen all too frequently up here, by the looks of the rocks at the side of the road.

Still, we keep climbing higher and higher into a landscape so treacherous and remote that people call it "The Roof of the World." Legend says that somewhere in these Himalayan Mountains lies a paradise called Shangri-La, and more than one village has erected a sign pointing to it: THIS WAY TO SHANGRI-LA!

We're almost there. And the closer we get, the more my thoughts keep flipping back to that *famous* phone call. My mother answered it. During the funeral, of all places, while we were standing around the grave. I couldn't believe it.

Escape

I t had to be bad news, the way she clutched her scarf to her throat as she listened, as if someone else had dropped dead. People were glaring at her. I nudged her.

"What is it?" I whispered.

The look in her eye—*yikes!*—maybe someone really *had* croaked. What else would make her walk away from her Aunt Gretchen's grave? And keep walking, almost at a run, all the way to the parking lot. I wanted to escape with her, but that clueless minister was droning on about "Gretchen's loving granddaughter," meaning me. Which proved how much he knew.

"—who, in spite of the pressures of her final exams, did so much to ensure this perfect farewell—"

I couldn't stand it. She wasn't my grandmother. She was my mother's aunt, which made her my great-aunt. My mean, bitter, grouchy great-aunt. Yes, I read a poem at the chapel, it's true, because I'd never had the opportunity to say goodbye to a family member. In fact, Aunt Gretchen was the only family we had, Mom and me. But the instant the ceremony ended, I tossed my bunch of lilacs on the coffin and hurried to join Maddy at the car. I saw her through the window hiding behind her veil, so I knocked, just to be safe. She opened the door.

"Hurry up and get in," she said, almost choking on tears. Real tears, I might add.

"What is it?" I asked.

"My father," she said, starting the engine.

"What father?"

"My goddamned father."

Sure, technically she did have a father, just like technically I also had a father. But they might as well have been dead. At least that's the attitude Maddy took to save her sanity.

"So why is he calling?" I asked.

"He's not."

"Oh. He's not dead, is he?"

"Not quite."

"What do you mean?"

"Coma. I can't believe it. We never hear from him and suddenly he's dying. What a joke." Her voice was bitter.

"Where is he?" I asked.

She lifted the veil and stepped on the accelerator before the funeral party could descend upon our car.

"I can't believe he's alive," I said. "Where does he live? How did he get our phone number?"

"He's in Greece," she snapped. "His lawyer wants me to come."

"What did you say?"

"What do you think I said?"

"I think you told him to f-off."

"Roxy, please!"

"You're not going, are you?"

Silence.

"Maddy?"

That's what I call my mother—Maddy. We never went in for the *mom* thing.

"If you think I intend to see that man, even if he *is* on his deathbed..."

The look she gave me for assuming she was going to Greece made me feel like an idiot. Obviously, she wasn't crazy about doing the *daughter* thing either. Her tears, though, made me wonder what was really going on inside her. Her father had abandoned her, God's truth—just walked away when she was a baby. Dumped her onto his sister, Gretchen. He had never contacted her, and now he was dying. The whole thing was making me sick to my stomach. As a matter of fact, I'd been feeling pretty crummy all week.

"What happened to him?" I asked.

"His head," she said.

"What about his head?"

"Brain damage or something."

"How?"

"Boat."

"It sunk?"

"They don't know what happened."

"How did the lawyer find you?" I asked.

She wasn't listening. I thought she was going to break the steering wheel off. "If anyone thinks I'm going to Greece to take care of him after he left me like that..."

"And he didn't just leave you. He left you with *you know who*."

"'That selfish, narcissistic, pathetic man, James Bearsden...'" That was Maddy's Gretchen impersonation—the exact words Aunt Gretchen had often used to disparage her brother, whom she never forgave for dumping little Maddy on her. But Maddy's rant typically went on longer than that. She seemed to have run out of venom.

"You forgot *irresponsible* and *immature*," I said.

Maddy laughed.

"I don't see what's so funny," I said.

Her laughter turned into sniffles, and she brooded in silence all the way home.

For all her gazillion faults, Maddy wasn't such a bad person. But as mothers go, she was high maintenance, requiring infinite patience and compassion. Back in our apartment, I watched her at the kitchen bar as she nibbled designer salad mix, one bitter leaf at a time, out of a plastic bag.

"Excuse me, *Mother*," I said, as kindly as I could, "it seems to me that, despite everything, he's still...you know...your father."

I hadn't expected my voice to quaver and my eyes to prick with tears. I might have blamed the funeral for making me so edgy, but the truth is I'd been on the verge of tears all through my final exams.

I intercepted Maddy's feedbag so that she'd look at me, so I could search her face for some sign of compassion.

"And he *is* dying," I said, thinking maybe she should go to Greece to see the old man.

She snatched her lettuce back as if I'd stolen her stash of self-pity.

"Let me make you an omelette," I said, stepping over to the fridge for eggs, onions and tomatoes.

Maddy Hunter, the actor with the big red hair, collapsed into a chrome barstool, all arms and legs and leopard-skin spandex. I'm sorry to say that my mother is no beauty. Smoking had carved premature cracks in her face, and her neck is a mile too long. But her look gets her challenging roles that have earned her excellent reviews. A recent one praised her portrayal of a woman struggling to contain her inner monster. The reviewer wrote that he couldn't take his eyes off her for fear Maddy might kill herself. Of course, Maddy did have plenty of reasons to do exactly that, starting with a belief that she had killed her own mother, which, let's face it, she had done, in a manner of speaking. Can you imagine living with *that* your whole life?

I gave her an onion to chop, and she turned the task into an Academy Award-winning performance of a woman shredding the remains of her heart.

"I'm thinking Gretchen knew where her brother was all these years," she said.

"No!" I said. "And kept it from us? She'd have to be a psycho." I cracked some eggs and whisked them wildly. "Anyway, you don't know that. You can't know that," I said. She responded with a riff of aimless cleaver hacks. "You don't know that, Maddy," I repeated.

"I know it as much as a person can know something without actually knowing it," she said. It was neat the way she punctuated her argument with percussive chops. "He was her brother. Think about it," she added. "She must have known."

I had to admit, as ugly as the notion was, it was feasible. I turned on an element and started to sauté the onion.

"Okay," she said. "Okay, yes, you're right, someone should be there..."

I smiled at her and whisked the eggs some more. *This is good,* I thought.

Then I heard her mutter, "...when he dies."

Maddy picked up the cleaver again and began to julienne the hell out of some lettuce. I hurried to finish cooking the omelette.

"You should really be there *before* he dies," I suggested. "That would be the whole point." I could imagine a dramatic deathbed reconciliation scene.

"Well, I can't go, can I?" she snapped. "I'm busy."

That ticked me off, since I'd gone to the trouble of making her a damned omelette. So I stepped out onto the balcony where I always felt better, surrounded by my potted plants. The ornamental orange tree needed some serious TLC. Our cat had climbed it and broken off several branches in an attempt to get at its sour oranges, of which there were already precious few—just like our family, that stingy plant bore little fruit. The cat bit into one and had the runs for a week. I ran my fingertips over the splinted limbs. Tears blurred my eyes. I leaned on the balcony railing and stared through gaps in the high-rises to the mountains beyond. *Mountains of loneliness,* I thought, and felt anger at my pathetic family. My father, for example, last seen heading north to search for gold—or his sexual orientation, according to Maddy. Considered dead. And my grandmother— what had she done to deserve death by childbirth? Imagining her gruesome end made me break out in a sweat, since the same fate would probably await me if I were ever to have a child, which wasn't beyond the realm of possibility. In fact, during certain—*ahem*— sessions with my boyfriend, Doug, excuse me, my now *ex-boyfriend* Doug, I felt the family curse hovering over me like a vulture.

For a second, I imagined myself in Greece with my grandfather. I hated him, sure. What else could I feel after living with Maddy and Aunt Gretchen all my life? But after all, he *was* my grandfather. And I suddenly thought that it might be nice to have a real grandfather, even if he *was* half-dead. As I stood there in the darkness, twenty-one floors up, I realized for the first time how different we were, Maddy and me. She'd as soon chop down our family tree as give it a drink of water. Perhaps it was time I had my own space. As I stood there on the balcony, I could hear the umbilical cord breaking.

What I actually heard was a cork popping.

I turned to see Maddy in the kitchen pouring herself a commiserating glass of red wine. I slipped through the sliding doors to confront her.

"So I've decided—"

I stalled, but not because I was chickening out. No, quite the opposite. The urge to go to Greece was thundering through my veins like a herd of wild horses. It startled me how strongly I felt that I was doing the right thing.

"I'll go to Greece for you," I finally managed to say.

The look on her face! "Oh, darling, no, no, no." She was all terror and relief as she raised her glass to me. "My angel of mercy, are you sure?" She kissed me on the cheek and in the next breath said, "Well, let's think about it."

"I have," I said. "I'm going."

She hugged me, her heart pounding through that scrawny breastbone of hers. Then she stepped back and looked at me suspiciously.

"This is no holiday, Roxy," she said. "Greece is not your precious Shangri-La."

"Eat your omelette," I said. "It's getting cold."

"Sweetie, I've been thinking," she said.

It was the day before my flight. I'd been watching her getting more and more anxious all day, so I didn't like where this was going.

"About what?" I asked.

"You're going to wind up regretting this."

"I'm going," I said.

"No, Roxy, I've changed my mind. I have a horrible feeling that Aunt Gretchen was right. A broken heart is all that can come of this—of going to him."

"I'll risk it," I said.

"No, sweetie, it's settled. I would never forgive myself."

"For what?"

"Trip's off, okay? It was never on. What was I thinking? Go have a nice summer. Meet a boy. Get a tattoo or something. Have fun. My God, you're only seventeen once! I wish I were seventeen again. I'd sure do things differently. Just you be careful."

We *had* been careful, Doug and I. No way was *I* going to be one of those girls huddled in the bathroom worrying about a missed period. Wait a second! A missed period? *Oh, my God. What day is it? The twenty-third?* I'd missed my period by a mile. What with Gretchen dying and everything, I'd completely spaced out about it. It wasn't unusual. Our bodies aren't like clockwork, but still—

Oh, my God! Is that why my breasts are tender? And why I feel like I have the flu? Don't tell me. Please, don't tell me.

"Roxy? What's the matter?" Maddy asked.

"Nothing," I said.

"Not nothing," she said. "I know you. What's wrong?"

I turned away. She *did* know me. Only too well. But she was the last person I'd tell, knowing how she'd react and what she'd want me to do about it. *Oh, my God.* If I *were* pregnant, the first thing I'd need to do is figure out how I felt about it. Without her bugging me. And here was a chance to get far away from her. *Greece is almost halfway around the world.*

"Maddy," I pressed, "the worst that's going to happen to me in Greece is that I wind up hating your father as much as you do."

"Exactly," she said.

"And how's that going to happen if he's in a coma?" She looked away. "Maddy? He *is* in a coma, isn't he?" She wouldn't look at me.

"So it's a little late to pretend we're the happy little family," I said.

"Well, I *believe* in family," she said.

I'd never heard that before, and I would have asked her to repeat it, but it had squeaked so tentatively out of her mouth that I knew she wasn't acting. I kept quiet so that those words might echo in her head and, sure enough, a moment later she was giving me extra money to buy a dress for the funeral. Instead of a mourning outfit, I should buy something I wanted, she told me. Something white and summery.

Or a maternity dress!

It was too late to run to the pharmacy. In fact, it was time for bed. I listened to Maddy as she spoke long-distance to the lawyer who had agreed to look out for me during the week I'd be in Greece. Suddenly I was the one flip-flopping, wondering if jet travel was good for the—you know—the fetus. *The fetus!* But I would have an abortion, wouldn't I? That's how you dealt with a family curse. But first things first: I would buy a pregnancy kit at the airport before boarding the plane.

As I lay in bed, I kept thinking of Maddy saying she believed in family. But surely Maddy would want me to have an abortion. Was that what *I* wanted? All I could think about was my mother's real mother, Roxana Khan, who had died in childbirth at the very same age as I am now. And here I was, pregnant too.

Perhaps my life as I knew it was over.

Roxy, what the hell have you done!

3

Hungry Hearts

"Three minutes," the instructions said. I read them carefully three times as the plane took off, but had to wait until the seat belt sign went off before trekking up the aisle to the washroom.

First, one little blue line appeared on the strip, but that was okay, because if a second line didn't show, then I was negative. What agony, waiting! Then, unmistakably, a second blue line! I couldn't believe it, didn't want to believe it, but there it was: the pee in the plastic cup was yellow, the strip was blue, and my face in the mirror was white. I sat down again on that miserable little toilet in that cramped cubicle and cried until someone knocked on the door. The funny thing was, when I emerged I wanted to tell someone, anyone, that I was pregnant. How stupid was that? Hey, I'd just set a new benchmark for dumb: getting pregnant! I could not believe it. Mainly because I couldn't afford to believe it. And I wasn't finished with being a teenager yet.

I made my way on rubbery legs back to my seat, where the first thing I did was reread the instructions on the pregnancy kit, hoping I'd misread. But no such luck. I couldn't believe that people couldn't hear my heart pounding. How appropriate that a baby should be howling somewhere about twenty rows away. I couldn't tune it out, not until I started to compose my "Dear Doug" letter: *Hey, Dooger, you'll never guess what...*

Well, I had a whole week to write it, although I'd probably have to hire Interpol to find him and deliver it. I was less concerned about Maddy, since she would doubtlessly kill me in an instant, so why worry? No, it was Grandmother Roxana I most wanted to talk to. She who died for the cause; the person I conjure up in my daydreams whenever I'm in trouble.

I took her picture out of my wallet. It was a small snapshot, the one image of her we possessed. She and I were dead-ringers for each other, especially now that we were both...well, I was *almost* eighteen, and Grandma would be eighteen forever. She peered out from beneath her raw silk shawl, her eyes pale as a northern wolf's, blue like mine. The photo had a scent to it, a fruity bouquet from the time Maddy spilled aromatherapy oil on it. I fell asleep thinking of Roxana in an orchard, picking ripe summer fruit off the vine.

It was three a.m. when the plane landed in Corfu, with me almost psycho from a weird mix of excitement, exhaustion and worry. By then I barely knew who I was anymore. Pregnant! So I was glad Maddy had arranged for me to be picked up at the airport by my grandfather's lawyer, Mr. Moustaki. I had a printout of his happy fat face.

Nothing at the airport was familiar, not even the local alphabet, which looked like Russian to me. If I had screamed for help, nobody would have understood me. After claiming my orange suitcase, I looked around the terminal building for that Moustaki person. All that hassle to hire a chaperone, so where was he? Tour operators held up cards with names on them, none of them mine. I was the only one not climbing into a tour bus or taxi. If Mr. Moustaki didn't show up, I'd be screwed. I took my hat off, hoping to be more recognizable as a female, but my short hair didn't help. My black jeans and T-shirt were supposed to make me look thinner, but I felt downright invisible. It occurred to me that maybe I'd gotten on the wrong plane—maybe this was Istanbul. I felt like throwing up. Morning sickness, maybe.

"Nice hotel, miss, very cheap."

I spun around to see an unshaven character holding a grimy brochure.

"I take you, yes, please," he said. "Cheap hotel, cheap." He looked gaunt, hungry, almost derelict.

"I have a hotel, thank you," I said.

I was prepared to scream if he laid a hand on me. Then I saw the grey head of a kitten poking out of his jacket pocket. It was all too weird. I ran outside where a bus was pulling away in a cloud of sickly sweet diesel smoke, but that creepy guy was on my case again. "Miss! Miss!" Maddy would have told him to f-off. I shuddered to imagine her reaction if someone actually touched her.

"Excuse me," I said, turning away and pulling out my new cellphone, without which Maddy wouldn't let me leave home. But the man grabbed my elbow, and as I swung around, my carry-on flew off my shoulder and my phone hit the pavement.

"You have no idea how much this cost," I said.

That's when I realized he'd rescued my suitcase. Like an idiot, I must have set it down inside the terminal and forgotten it. Before I could apologize, a security guard motioned him to get into his car where a boy about five years old sat watching us through the window. What was a child doing up at three o'clock in the morning, I wondered.

"Miss Hunter!"

I turned to see a man waving at me from across the road. Huge relief. But no way this old guy was Mr. Moustaki; he didn't look anything like the photo.

He had difficulty getting out of the car. As he walked toward me, I could see that he couldn't straighten up. He was dressed in a crumpled khaki shirt and trousers, as if he'd just returned from safari.

"You are Miss Hunter, yes?" he asked with a German accent.

"You're not Mr. Moustaki," I snapped.

"No," he said, chuckling. Then the chuckle became a cough, which he stifled painfully, as if his ribs hurt. "My name is Oscar

Hartmann. Please, call me Oscar. Dimitris is conveying his apologies that he cannot be here to meet you personally, my dear."

"Who's Dimitris?" I asked.

So far, nothing added up. No way was I handing over my belongings to a strange old man at three o'clock in the morning.

"Dimitris Moustaki, the lawyer," he said. "Your mother employed him, I believe." He waved me to his car. "Please, you must be very tired."

Then he took my suitcase and opened the trunk of the car. But there was no room for it, because a slab of stone took up all the space. He looked embarrassed and slammed the trunk shut. But I know what a gravestone looks like. This one had been engraved with the image of a tree, and beneath it was an inscription:

The hungry heart leads home

This was getting way too weird.

It occurred to me, as I climbed into the back seat with my suitcase, that I might have arrived too late and the funeral was over. I thought of Maddy, since she'd made me promise, promise, promise to phone her from the cemetery. I think she wanted to hear the sound of dirt landing on the coffin.

"Excuse me," I said, "but this taxi doesn't have a meter. My mother warned me not to take a taxi that doesn't have a proper meter." I was starting to feel very ill. "I should warn you, sir, I have no money."

"My dear, I have no money either," he chuckled. "For this, I have learned to be thankful."

What an oddly pleasant man, I thought.

We sped toward town, entering a maze of narrow dark and deserted streets at full speed. Pools of amber streetlight splashed around the interior of the car, along with a blast of warm night air. I was getting dizzier by the minute.

"Where's Mr. Moustaki?" I shouted over the engine noise.

Since Oscar couldn't turn his head, I had to lean forward, but all I heard was "Athens," and "terrible" and "delayed," and I wondered if Mr. Moustaki had been in an accident.

"He's okay, isn't he?" I asked.

"Your grandfather?"

Yeah, my dead grandfather, I thought, *whose gravestone is in the trunk of the car.*

"Jim is going to make it," Oscar said.

My heart skipped a beat. "He is?"

Oscar was watching me in the mirror, curious about something. "Why are you staring at me?" I asked.

"Please, excuse me, but I can see Jim in your face, in your expression."

"I wouldn't know," I said. "I've never met him. We've only heard about him."

"I suppose you have heard things," he said.

"Not much. But enough."

"You will excuse me for talking so frankly," he said, "and so late at night, but I must inform you that your grandfather did *not* wish to die."

As if someone said he did? He wished to die?

My heart was racing. "I thought it was an accident," I said.

Oscar paused a fraction of a second too long, so that when he said, "Of course it was an accident," how could I be expected to believe him?

I could see my hotel up ahead—the Oasis. The headlights lit up a sinister circle of cats around the front door; an evil omen if I'd ever seen one. No light on either, the windows all shuttered tight, and the same eerie scene up and down both sides of the street. Oscar gave a little honk as we blew right by it, thank goodness.

"Oasis is crap," he said. "I know from deeply personal experience. I will find you a better place."

Alarm bells were going off in my head. A strange man was taking me God knows where, my phone was in pieces, and I was pregnant and exhausted.

We didn't speak again until he stopped at the Arcadian. Oscar chattered away in Greek with the concierge, explaining who I was,

I guess, which seemed to wake the guy up. After I was given a key, Oscar promised to come by once I'd gotten some sleep.

"I can probably find the hospital by myself," I said.

"But, my dear, your grandfather was discharged."

"No way."

"He is home now, a week already, oh yes."

"I thought he was in a coma," I said.

"Yes, well, he woke up. I was there. Straight away, he said to me, he said, 'Oscar, are we in heaven?' I said, 'Jim, they wouldn't let you in.' He said, 'Why not?' 'Because, Jim, you have left too much unfinished business here in this world.'"

I wanted to laugh, but Oscar was as serious as oatmeal. Then he collected my hand in his and with a little bow said, "*Guten nacht.*"

He turned and limped away.

He was right about my grandfather. There certainly was unfinished business.

A room full of blinding light, sick headache, not feeling rested at all. The conveyor belt in my brain didn't stop moving all night, sluicing and sorting through everything that had happened recently. Pregnant! Strange country! Completely alone! My grandfather trying to kill himself—was it true? Oscar insisting otherwise had only proved that it was. But why had he done it?

Only nine o'clock. I shut the window against the street noise and saw a shop owner rolling up his window blinds. The clatter sent pigeons exploding out of their roosts, and that's when I saw a horizontal strip of the sea above the roofline. The Mediterranean— at last! And up the street, a sidewalk cafe under stone arcades. This was more like the Europe I'd been expecting.

Since my grandfather was no longer on his deathbed, I felt free to hang out with a cappuccino and contemplate what a responsible person does with a baby.

Pregnant! I still couldn't believe it.

Two flights of curving marble steps took me down to the small lobby where a pleasant-looking woman at the desk greeted me with *"Kali mera."*

"Kali mera," I answered.

Once outside on the sidewalk, I saw Oscar at the curb, supporting himself on his open car door, arguing with someone. No way to slip away unseen.

"Miss Hunter!" Oscar shouted.

It was the other man who hurried toward me with his hand outstretched. I recognized him from the photo as Mr. Moustaki. He had a balding head, dark blue blazer and a white belt holding up a well-to-do belly.

"Very pleased to meet you, Miss Hunter," he said. Despite his warm handshake and tanned happy face, he seemed anxious. "You are tired after your long trip," he said.

Oh, great. I must look like a train wreck.

I nodded in agreement.

"My apologies for last night," he said. "By rights, your mother should fire me."

"What she doesn't know won't hurt her," I said.

"Very good," he said, greatly relieved.

"I keep her in the dark as much as possible," I said. "For her own good."

"I can see you are a considerate young woman."

I liked Mr. Moustaki immediately. "My mother doesn't even know her father is better," I said. "She wouldn't have sent me if she'd known."

"I'm sure I told your mother," he said. "Yes, quite sure."

"You did! She *knew* he was out of the hospital!"

I was stunned. She had known, and had sent me anyway!

"I explained to her on the phone, of course."

I felt my jaw drop.

"Secrets run in our family," I said. "We're quite dysfunctional."

Mr. Moustaki chuckled, but I wasn't joking.

"I promise you, my dear," he said, "your week in Corfu will be trouble free from now on. I will show you the sights. You must see Saint Spyridon's tomb."

I didn't dare dampen his enthusiasm. Museums bored me to tears. He looked at his watch.

"Have you eaten breakfast, Miss Hunter? It's an hour and a half drive to Afionas. Your grandfather is expecting you."

"Afionas?"

"Your grandfather's village. You'll be staying at the taverna. Jim is still recovering, so you cannot stay with him." He turned to Oscar. "A week with his granddaughter will do Jim some good!"

The look on Oscar's face: in all my life I'd never seen anyone so unsure about anything. I wasn't so sure myself about spending a week with my grandfather. Quite frankly, it terrified me. But Mr. Moustaki told me to go pack my bag while he got me a coffee and a sweet roll. When I reappeared downstairs, Oscar and Mr. Moustaki were arguing again.

"You are driving nowhere this morning," Mr. Moustaki said, "except to the doctor."

"It is no problem for me to drive Miss Hunter."

"Don't speak nonsense, Hartmann. Look at you." Moustaki turned to me. "That man should be in hospital."

It was true. You'd think Oscar had been shot through the heart, the way he favoured his rib cage.

"Taxi!" Mr. Moustaki shouted, but it passed without stopping.

"I am ready to go this very minute!" Oscar insisted.

"To the doctor you are going!" Moustaki said. Then, shaking his head, he turned to me. "Hartmann saved your grandfather's life, my dear, but look at him—I think he has broken a few ribs."

"You saved my grandfather?" I asked.

I could tell Oscar wasn't expecting any medals for it, from the way he muttered his response.

"I can show you newspaper articles, my dear," Moustaki said, "about how he breathed life into Jim's lungs. So, please, Hartmann!" he said, turning to him. "Don't speak such nonsense."

"You really should go to the doctor," I said.

"We will waste the whole day arguing with this stubborn old German," Moustaki said, looking at his watch. "I am late for court." He turned on Oscar again. "Drive carefully, for God's sake! If something happens to her, I will never forgive you."

Mr. Moustaki ushered me to his car, reached in through a window and grabbed a book.

"You will be so kind as to deliver this to your grandfather, yes?" He smelled it before handing it to me. "Fresh from the printer, his latest novel, now in five languages. He keeps me busy going to the bank." I must have looked surprised, because he added, "Oh yes, your grandfather is a very famous man over here."

The book was in German, so I couldn't understand the title, but I recognized the words "Alexander der Grosse" on the back cover. The author was someone called James Penman. I found his photo on the inside flap and studied it. Maddy had one picture of her father, and this was the same man, though much older. His hair had gone white, except for the beard, and he wore a contemplative scowl.

Once Mr. Moustaki had driven off in his old Mercedes, Oscar opened the book and showed me the dedication page. That old German's eyes welled up with tears.

> For my friend Oscar:
> Bless his hungry heart.

The hungry heart again, only this time it was Oscar's. Was the grave marker his? It made sense in a dark and twisted sort of way, but how totally goth, driving around with your own tombstone in the trunk of your car. He closed the book and handed it back to me, and that's when I saw his name on the cover: "Translated into German by Oscar Hartmann."

"Afionas, 125 kilometres," Oscar said, installing his broken body, limb by limb, behind the wheel. "Fasten your seat belt."

• • •

A veil of cloud softened the sun as Oscar took the coastal road out of Corfu town. Out on the water, a wind was whipping the waves into a bad mood. Or maybe it was just me who was in a bad mood, tired and anxious and suddenly in need of more sleep. I said nothing for five minutes, my mind back there in the trunk of the car with that tombstone.

"I'm not usually so moody," I said.

"Don't worry yourself about it," Oscar said. "You are still young. When you're as old as me, you can count on being grouchy every day."

I'd never met anyone like Oscar, so pleasant and pessimistic at the same time. Even with small talk. He liked to make something out of it and twist it around until you were left scratching your head.

"I'm nervous about meeting my grandfather," I said.

"He is more nervous, I assure you of that," Oscar said.

"I'm not surprised. When he sees a ghost from the past, he's gonna wish he was back in his coma." The look on Oscar's face convinced me that I'd hit the nail on the head. "The truth is, Mr. Hartmann, I didn't come here to make things better. Anyway, I wouldn't have a clue where to start."

"Good," he said. "Your grandfather has no use for do-gooders. Another reason he and I are such good friends."

"You saved his life," I said. "You can't be a better friend than that."

"Oh yes, I could," he said. "I could betray him." I didn't have a clue what he was talking about. "I could renege on my promise. You may tell him that."

"What promise?" I asked.

"My apologies for even mentioning it," he said.

I decided to give it a rest so Oscar could concentrate on his driving.

Besides, I got distracted by my first good look at Corfu. We'd climbed high into the hills. In almost every direction there were nothing but olive trees, all silvery green.

"Wow," I said. "It's like Corfu is covered with a lumpy old quilt."

Oscar looked out the window, as if that was news to him. "You should be a writer, like your grandfather," he said, looking at me intently.

Being compared with that man. *Whoa...*Thinking that we had something in common, something I could be proud of—it felt like I was betraying Maddy and all that she'd been through.

"I could write a story, Mr. Hartmann, believe me, I could."

"Then you must," he said. "You must be a writer!" He veered across the centre line.

"Mr. Hartmann!"

"What?"

"You make it sound like writing's a matter of life and death."

The look on his face—he actually believed it! Being a writer was the last thing I'd imagined for myself. There I was thinking I was going to be a social worker—going extreme and working in the slums of Calcutta.

I could write about that, I thought. "Okay, I'll write, if you just drive."

"Is that a promise?"

"No," I said.

He laughed. What a great old guy.

"May I ask why you're carrying around a gravestone?"

I could see him concocting an answer, but then he began blinking back tears.

"Is it my grandfather's?" I asked.

"Jim and I, we bought it on sale." He laughed again, which made him wince.

"Was it, like, second-hand or something?" I said, which started me laughing too. It was a crazy idea.

"First one in the ground wins the thing!" he shouted. "I was all ready to transport the damned thing to his funeral!" He could barely breathe for laughing, so I forced myself to stay silent, which only made me wonder about what Oscar wasn't telling me.

"I think I know what his secret is," I said. Oscar looked at me, alarmed. "Watch where you're going!" I shouted.

"You know?" His forehead crinkled up into a criss-cross of concern.

"Of course I know, Mr. Hartmann. He abandoned his daughter."

Oscar looked relieved. "You most certainly will remind him of that."

The other coastline soon came into view. Oscar said that, if not for the storm clouds blotting out the view, I would have been able to see all the way to Italy.

The downward journey began. It took a lot longer to wind our way back and forth along potholed roads through older and darker and more magnificent olive trees that overhung the road. Every tree had a billion silky leaves, each one a short silvery brushstroke like in a Van Gogh painting.

We sped through narrow villages perched on the steep sides of ridiculously scenic valleys. We must have been in the ancient part of Corfu, unchanged since before cars were invented, and to navigate the tightest curves Oscar had to make a wide arc that flirted with the edge of the cliff. I couldn't look.

"What's my grandfather's book about?" I asked, trying to distract myself.

"It's about the greatest Greek of all—Alexander. You have heard of him?"

"Of course. Alexander the Great. I wrote an essay in school about what a bully he was."

"I'm sure the United Nations would agree with you," he said.

"When he invaded Asia," I said, "he married a woman named Roxana. I suppose you know that."

"I do, indeed," Oscar said.

"That's also my grandmother's name," I said. "She came from the Himalayan Mountains in Kashmir, near Shangri-La. Did you know that?"

"Your grandfather is clever like that, always writing his own story in disguise."

"Isn't a novel supposed to be fiction?"

"The best literature contains a most wonderful code, my dear.

They may be flights of fancy, yet absolutely true in the way the characters make you feel. A good character can make you feel like crying for forgiveness for your own sins. Your grandfather has made his readers cry many times."

He made Maddy cry more than a few times, but I wasn't going to ruin the car ride by opening that can of worms. I started leafing through the pages, but of course they were all in German, so I could only imagine what the book was about.

"Just wondering," I said, "but does my grandfather, in his own mind, think he's Alexander the Great?"

Oscar swerved to pass a farmer puttering along on a homemade motorbike pulling a rickety trailer overloaded with firewood.

How totally quaint. And dangerous!

"Excuse me?" he said.

"My grandfather, he must think a lot of himself if he sees himself as Alexander."

"As a matter of fact, before he became a writer, your grandfather set out to conquer the world."

"Oh, please, Mr. Hartmann."

"I tell you, it's true. He brought remote parts of the world out of the Dark Ages."

"By doing what exactly?"

"Giving them electricity, my dear. He was an electrical engineer."

"In Asia?" I asked.

"In the Himalayan Mountains, they treated him like royalty."

It occurred to me that my grandfather had somehow met Roxana on his travels. I mean, I had no idea how she got to Scotland. Seriously, if that's what had happened, if he'd picked her up on his travels like a souvenir, I didn't want to know about it. And God help us if Maddy found out about it.

"All I know is that they were in Scotland when my grandmother got pregnant," I said. "I guess I shouldn't complain, since the baby was my mother." I was getting annoyed with Oscar staring at me as if he was probing my brain. "What?" I asked.

He averted his eyes, returning his gaze to the road.

"My grandmother died," I said. "I guess you know. That's not in the book, is it?"

He didn't answer, because we were slowing down as we approached a village. I sat bolt upright.

"Are we here?"

I'd imagined a fishing village, but we were high up on a peninsula. You could see the water a long way down, and a huge sky that was quickly becoming ugly. There was no hotel that I could see, just a couple of *tavernas*. Not really what you'd call a town, and there weren't many people around. Nobody who looked like Jim Bearsden Penman.

"Stefanos Taverna," Oscar said, nodding to his left. "I don't recommend for you to eat there on your own."

So what did he do but park directly in front of Stefanos, where three waiters were hauling tables off the patio before the rain hit. They were dressed identically in white shirts and black trousers. My eyes widened. Let's just say the scenery had improved considerably. Not that I was interested—I was *so* the opposite of interested. Anyway, those Greek god types were always too aware of their own charms. No, definitely *not* interested.

"You are staying over there, Miss Hunter." Oscar pointed across the road to the Kalypso Taverna.

The youngest of those waiters, who was about my age, ran to help Oscar out of the car. The way he attended to Mr. Hartmann's feeble condition without cringing made it seem as if they knew each other well. Once on his feet, Oscar studied him critically and uttered something that made the waiter run his hand sheepishly over his razor-sharp military haircut. His embarrassed smile said a lot about him.

"Georgio, this is Miss Hunter. Be a gentleman and show her to the Kalypso across the street. But first help me to the little boy's room."

"I, Georgio, will take you," he said, pronouncing the g's so it sounded more like *Yoryo*. "Please, one minute," he said. "I take Mr. Hartmann to my father's taverna. You wait, yes?"

I would wait all right, if only to get another look at those chocolate brown eyes of his. Not that I was interested. Hey, I was pregnant for God's sake! What was I thinking? So off they went, leaving me alone to chew my fingernails and listen to the wind whistling through the church belfry as thunder rumbled overhead.

So this was my grandfather's Greek paradise? Talk about a dead end. No question about it being the end of the road, complete with a tree standing in the middle of a small whitewashed concrete roundabout. Everything in the village was whitewashed—the church with its twin bell towers, the houses, the tavernas, even the bottom six feet of the tree trunk. The whole village looked like it was made of meringue.

A priest appeared in the church doorway, bearded and black-frocked, watching to see what the wind blew in. Ditto an old lady in her widow black, who stopped on her way up a side street and stood there like a statue. One old man at Stefanos Taverna sat at a patio table, still as death, ignoring the coming storm. A horror writer would have loved this place, especially Stefanos' entrance arch laced with dead vines that rattled in the wind. It made me sad, since plants don't need much attention—just a little coaxing once in a while—and it bothered me all out of proportion to things I should have been worrying about, like a) being pregnant, and b) meeting my grandfather.

I noticed two girls, about twelve years old, appearing from a narrow lane beyond the roundabout. They stopped when they saw me, then continued their approach. They were bold little creatures, marching right up to the car and saying, "Hello!" and, "How are you?" very sing-songy, like they'd had it drilled into them by some choirmaster.

"How are you?" I asked, getting out of the car.

"Very well," they said in unison. "We are very modern girls."

Modern girls in a very old village, I thought.

"Is there an old man living here named James Bearsden?" I asked.

I might have been an alien, the way they gawked at me, until it dawned on them. "Oh, Uncle Jim!" They pointed up the lane down which they'd come.

Uncle Jim? Meaning what exactly? That my grandfather had more family?

"He lives up that lane?"

They made great big arm gestures, as in, *keep going*.

"How far?"

"Too late," they said.

"No too late!" It was the waiter with the boot camp haircut.

"Too late, too late!" the girls shouted.

"No too late!" Georgio said. "Hey, I take you, yes? Come on! Wait here!" He ran to the church and disappeared through the heavy wooden doors.

"Too late," the girls insisted, as if they knew and nobody else did.

"Why too late?" I asked, suddenly alarmed. "Has something happened to Jim?"

While the girls assembled their next sentence, Georgio emerged from the church on a red motorbike, tinny engine screaming and that scrawny priest in pursuit. I didn't like what was happening, and Oscar was nowhere to be seen.

"Let's go!" the boy said.

Lightning tore a hole in the clouds overhead, followed by a deafening *kaboom*. I wasn't going anywhere.

"Where's Oscar?" I asked.

The priest caught up and grabbed hold of the handle bars. He obviously didn't want Georgio making off with his putt-putt. I noticed that the priest couldn't take his spooky eyes off me, as if I had horns growing out of my head.

"Miss Hunter!"

It was Oscar, limping toward me. He pulled a little box from his shirt pocket and pressed it discreetly into my hands, whispering, "For Jim. Please give it to him when you and he are alone." He winked.

Of all the weird things, on the front of the cardboard box I read: "Smith Corona -Typewriter Ribbon." I stuffed it into my purse.

"My dear," he said. "I'm afraid I must return to town." He looked really crappy, poor guy. "Father Katadodis will show you to your grandfather's."

"Is too late," the priest said.

"No too late!" Georgio insisted.

"For God's sake!" Oscar shouted. "Miss Hunter has travelled halfway around the world to meet her grandfather. Will one of you please take her the last mile!"

The next thing I knew the scrawny priest was on the bike's saddle and, as we roared away, I clung to him for dear life.

Up a meandering lane we sped, bouncing and dodging disintegrating bits of concrete sidewalk until we'd left the houses behind and were flying past chicken coops and garden patches and then into open fields of rock and prickly low shrubs. Something smelled incredibly fragrant. The wind carried pellets of rain that stung my face, so I hid behind the priest's robe, which billowed out like an airbag. We scooted gently downhill along the narrowing central ridge of the peninsula. When we stopped, we were still fifty feet above the sea. What next? Leave the bike and scramble down dangerous-looking stone steps to the beach? Not me.

We got off the bike. It wasn't quite the end of the peninsula. At the bottom of the escarpment, a sandy neck of land led to a few final acres of rock—almost an island but not quite. A lone house sat out there, cut off from civilization by waves that threatened to crash over that frail isthmus. It was wild and idyllic. And incredibly remote—perfect if you were hiding from something. But there was no way, on account of those waves, that we were going across. Not a chance.

"Too late," the priest said, throwing his hands up in frustration.

"You mean, too late because of the storm?" I said. It had started to pour rain.

He nodded. "Uncle Jim—he is your grandfather?" He sounded like he wanted proof of it.

"Yes!" I had to yell over the wind, and it felt like I was trying to prove it to myself. "Yes!"

"I think you can help me."

"Help with what?"

It didn't seem to bother him that we were getting soaked. "He is no Orthodox," he said.

"Orthodox?"

"The Greek church. Very important we bring him into the church," he said.

"On Sunday?"

"Every Sunday, yes! Until the wedding."

"*Wedding!*"

The priest raised a hand to shield his face against the rain, and pointed to the house on the not-so-distant rocks. "To schoolteacher. There!"

I saw a woman run from the house into the storm to gather laundry off a clothesline. A tall man stood under a trellis that covered the entrance to the house, supporting himself with a cane. When the priest kick-started the engine back to life, the man looked our way. I couldn't take my eyes off him as I climbed back onto the bike. There he was. I could hardly believe it. It was somehow perfect, the way he stood there, defiant, as the gods raged above him. He was probably happiest just like that, cut off from everything. The last thing I saw through the pouring rain was a goat nudging my grandfather, trying to reach shelter on the patio, but that billy goat got himself a cruel whack on the head just for thinking about it.

We bolted back to the village, with lightning sizzling across the sky just over our heads, and then crashing with such force that I felt my heart jump. I could smell it, it was that close. Were the gods angry at me? Who knew what they wanted? Maybe they were snarly because I had taken cover behind a priest. Then, brooding over their bad luck, the gods tossed their next bolt half a mile out to sea, making the water smoke. I couldn't believe it.

Don't be frightened, Roxy. Think of the safest place deep inside you. Think of Grandma Roxana Khan.

• • •

The priest dropped me off at the taverna. The woman who ran it had lamb stew waiting for me, deliciously cinnamon tasting, with tons of little onions in it. Her name was Xenia. The waiter who worked across the street, the one who wanted to take me to see my grandfather, sat at my table watching me eat. For paying attention to me, he got a gold star, but his smelling vaguely of fish nearly cancelled out my attraction to him.

4

Odysseus

My most restless night in living memory started with screams that sounded like a baby being murdered. I got up to close the clattering shutters and found a tomcat on my balcony, its back arched. My eyes were open for hours after that, warding off night terrors. I woke again at seven to be sick, then returned to bed with the shivers, wanting Maddy there to stroke my head like she used to. Having a baby was starting to seem every bit the dumb idea I'd always imagined it to be. Next thing I knew it was eleven o'clock, the day nearly half over. Pulling a pillow over my head, I could still hear the window shutters rattling like a typewriter. *Grrrr.*

Maddy would be waiting for a call.

Back home, it was...earlier or later? My brain hurt, trying to figure it out. I'd travelled east to get to Greece, so Vancouver was west, farther from the rising sun, so back home it was still last night. Maddy would be up. I should phone her. And tell her what exactly? "Oh, by the way, Mother, I'm pregnant." *Good for you, dear.* That's what I hoped she'd say, since that's how she'd brought me up. "Mom, I'm running away." *Good for you, dear.* "Mom, I'm going to be a hooker." *Good for you, dear.* It's clever, when you think about it, because she didn't mean it, and she knew that I knew that she didn't mean it, but just the sound of it made me feel grown-up, like my decisions were mine and nobody else's. And the consequences too.

Exactly. The consequences.

In any event, I wasn't going to tell her. Yet.

Eleven thirty and I was starving. I opened the window and pushed back the wooden shutters to find the sky a ragged mess. Out on the horizon, a lonely family of bare black rocks sat all in a row, like humps on a dragon's back. But the steep hillside below me was as pretty as a fairy tale, with its small terraced plots full of olive trees.

It was almost noon when I grabbed my purse and found my way downstairs to the dining room. I had my eye out for a computer so I could email my friends back home. No luck. Only six old women dressed in black who turned their heads in unison to fix their gaze upon me. I thought I'd interrupted a funeral. They sat at tables without so much as a coffee cup between them. Xenia appeared from the kitchen in a green and white floral dress and a green silk scarf over her head. She looked like a long-ago movie star. "Kali mera!" she said, all sunny.

"Good morning," I said.

"In Greek," she insisted.

"Kali mera," I amended.

"Bravo!" she said.

She coaxed me to say it again to the village women who continued to stare so rudely. One or two of them made an effort to reciprocate.

"I need to phone home," I told Xenia.

She showed me to one of those clunky old-fashioned black rotary phones attached to a wall, told me how to dial direct to Canada and then disappeared into the kitchen. If it was noon in Greece, it was three o'clock in the morning in Vancouver—roughly Maddy's bedtime.

"It's about time you called," she said when she picked up.

"Sorry," I said. The phone cord was no longer than my arm, making privacy impossible unless I turned my back on the room. "I just woke up," I whispered.

"I've been calling your cellphone—why haven't you picked up?"

"Um, well, the reception's probably not so good here." I didn't want to mention the broken phone.

"Have you seen him yet?" she asked.

"You knew he wasn't dying, Maddy, and you sent me anyway."

"Yes, I did. Do you know why? I may as well tell you. You won't believe this."

"What?"

"Before you left, I found my father's address in Gretchen's will. She *did* know where he was."

"What! That's...that's..."

"I know! I know! Just calm down. Tell me something. Have you seen him?"

"No, not really. But he's writing books, I know that much, and making a lot of money."

"How much?"

"I don't know, but I'll ask *the schoolteacher he's marrying*."

"He's not!" she said, as if by her command it could be stopped.

"People do it all the time, Maddy," I said.

"How could he? He's an old man. Does he know what he's doing?" I could hear her panicking.

"I don't know, Mom, I just got here."

"Well, please make it your business to know. And do something about it. He's been in a coma. He's not in his right mind, isn't it obvious?"

"I don't know about *obvious*, but it's *possible*," I said.

"Why? What have you heard?"

I'd said enough, knowing how Maddy could blow things out of proportion, especially something like suicide, so I used the excuse of Xenia arriving with my breakfast to say goodbye and hang up.

Yoghurt with honey, doughnut holes drizzled with honey, a hard-boiled egg, thick slices of white bread, a small bowl of olives and a cup of black tea. With honey. I began to wolf it down, which amused Xenia, but not that jury of crones who sat grim-faced as ever.

"Are they, like, the Afionas welcoming committee?" I asked Xenia.

She smiled nervously, and shook her head as she whispered, "*Oh-khee*," meaning no.

Then she pulled a chair up close. "We did not know Jim has a family," she whispered. "It is a surprise for everyone."

I kept eating, trying to suppress my sarcastic urges. Then something occurred to me. "You're not the schoolteacher, are you?"

"Me?" She blushed. "Oh-khee! We have Miss Skandalidis," she said, proudly, pointing toward the village. "Just there, at the school."

"She's there now?"

She looked at her watch and nodded, and at the same time her expression changed.

"No summer holidays in Greece?" I asked.

"No holidays for children who want to speak English," she said, then turned abruptly to wave away a gaggle of preschoolers who were leaving greasy finger marks on her window. "Go home!" she yelled, charging outside.

On her way back inside, she spoke to the old crows, who then started to file out. Xenia sat down again, and I could tell by her self-conscious pause that she was about to take a huge load off her mind.

"Uncle Jim is going to marry our Danda," she said. "Danda Skandalidis."

"I know, the priest told me. But my grandfather isn't Orthodox. I guess that's a big problem."

"That is a problem of Father Katadodis," she said. "For Danda the problem is..." She whispered the next bit, even though we were alone in the dining room. "He is still married?"

"My grandfather? No, that was centuries ago. My grandmother died a long time ago."

She looked only somewhat relieved. "But still, this is a surprise. Do you understand? A man who asks a woman to marry him does not keep secrets like that."

He hadn't mentioned his family? Xenia was right—how can you trust somebody who keeps his past a secret? She took my hand in hers and said, "Please, yes, go and meet her. Before she meets you."

The school was only a minute away. I hoped to sneak up and catch a close up of Danda before *she met me*. The way Xenia put it, she sounded dangerous. Her students spotted me immediately, since the school sat like a temple on a rise of land and the kids were hanging out on the steps.

When I reached the open doorway, I saw a woman standing beside her desk, in silhouette. Sunlight from a window behind her burst through her dress like X-rays showing her mature curves perfectly suited to having half a dozen children at least. Thick wavy hair fell to just above her shoulders in the style of foreign correspondents reporting from someplace like Cairo or Buenos Aires. One fist rested on her hip, like she meant business. It was a pose I would have to practice; seriously, it was impressive. It seemed to me she must have been as nervous as I was, because she popped a pill and chased it with bottled water.

I knocked.

"Hey! Hi. I'm Roxy."

She marched toward me, no hesitation at all, shooing kids out of the room as she went as if striding through a chicken coop. Up close, I could see by her strained smile how stressed out she was.

"I am Danda Skandalidis," she said, extending her hand to me. Her grip was strong and cool, but *mine* was like ice.

It was hate at first sight.

"You know about me?" I asked, through gritted teeth.

"Oh yes."

I took that to mean *barely.* It was clear that my arrival had *not* been expected.

"Why Jim's sister did not tell us about your visit?" she asked.

"You know my Aunt Gretchen?" I wondered how that was even remotely possible.

"Jim speaks of her, of course," she said.

That meant Danda had known about Gretchen without knowing about Maddy and me. Our family was more screwed up than I'd ever imagined.

She quickly ushered me out of the school and shut the door—well, more like slammed. I wasn't surprised that she was upset—imagine finding out that the man you're going to marry has a family you knew nothing about. I was trying to get my head around Gretchen being in touch with her brother and keeping it a secret from us. I was so furious that I couldn't carry on a polite conversation.

"So you know she's dead," I said, sharply.

"Dead?"

"Yes. Three weeks ago."

"I'm sorry." Danda's face softened.

"Don't be. We hated her."

Danda seemed not to know how to respond to that. "We should not tell Jim yet, in any case. He's too fragile, and we should not give him bad news. Come, I will take you to see him. Today is for good news, yes?"

Me? Did she mean *I* was good news? I hadn't gotten that impression. But all of a sudden, we were on our way to meet him, passing the church and proceeding up that meandering lane that wound its way out the back end of the village. This time, I could appreciate the rustic little doorways and window boxes, all bleached blue and full of flowers.

"It is beautiful here in Afionas, yes?" Danda said.

"Well, it's off the beaten track," I said, "if you like that sort of thing."

"I love that sort of thing," she said. "I am from Athens. Ugh!"

"You must really love my grandfather's place," I said, my sarcasm leaking all over the place. "It's like the end of the world."

"Men like Jim must have their independence," she said.

Getting married sounds like a great way to keep your independence, I thought, and I might have blurted it out if two boys hadn't come running up from behind, double-teaming a wicker basket. Danda intercepted them, folded back the linen cover to reveal apples, lemons, croissants, buns and a Thermos. The aroma of freshly baked bread was to die for.

"You can see how we are helping your grandfather back to health," she said, brushing a hand over one boy's unkempt hair before taking charge of the basket and releasing them to return to the village. I watched them as they ran. They bumped into Xenia who approached carrying empty plastic bottles.

She and Danda chatted in Greek as we kept walking, until Xenia stopped in the doorway of a dark shed and began filling a bottle with red wine from a massive wooden barrel.

"Things are going to change in Afionas. This village is so backward," Danda said.

"Danda will teach our daughters to be modern women," Xenia explained. "Greek girls marry too young."

Danda beamed.

"A girl needs a strong mind to match to her strong body," Danda said. "Only then, if she wants to, should she get married and have children. Don't you agree, Roxy?"

"I guess," I said.

"I swear on my mother's grave," Danda said, "Greece will know Afionas as the home of powerful women."

"And all because of your grandfather," Xenia announced, as she capped a second bottle and headed back, leaving Danda and me to continue on our way.

"What's my grandfather got to do with it?" I asked Danda.

"Jim is building a new school."

"He is?"

"We will even get new computers," Danda said with a huge grin.

"Just computers?" I said. "If you want modern girls, they'll need more than that." Danda stopped to better hear me out. "They'll need broadband Internet," I said, "and maybe even enough wireless routers to connect the whole village. And scanners and webcams and the latest software. I could even download some great free stuff for you." Danda was staring at me, like, *Where did this chick get her Ph.D.?* "They can build their own website and start a blog," I said. "I could show them how to do that too, if you want."

Danda's face lit up. In fact, her whole demeanor changed, and she gently wiped something from my cheek—probably egg. I was sorry I'd said anything.

Beyond the chicken coops and piles of flattened plastic water bottles at the outskirts of the village, we arrived at open fields of wild herbs: oregano, thyme and rosemary. You couldn't walk without kicking low-lying bushes and sending up an aura of perfume. But it wasn't enough to make me forget where I was headed.

As the peninsula narrowed, more and more sea came into view on each side of the ridge until land's end was in sight, with my grandfather's house sitting alone on the rocks. I'd seen calendars with photos of houses like his, snow-white cubes with impossibly blue seas in the background. The windows were sunk deep into thick walls and shaded by a trellis covered with red bougainvillea.

Danda stopped when we reached the top of the escarpment that led down to the beach, and from that vantage point she shaded her eyes to survey the two little bays below. The waves had calmed, but the storm had left a small lagoon in the middle of the sandy isthmus, making the connection even more tenuous.

"Do you study *The Odyssey* in school?" she asked, sounding doubtful.

"Of course," I said. Although whether I *remembered* anything was another question.

"You know how Odysseus was shipwrecked in a storm," she said.

Hmmm. Shipwrecked? It seemed to be a theme around here.

"This is where it happened," she said, "where Odysseus the warrior was found, nearly drowned."

"No way," I said.

"It was on that beach." She pointed to the small bay on the western side of the isthmus. "The winds blow from that direction, all the way from Italy. Princess Nausicaa, she found Odysseus here, wrapped in the sail of his boat. She nursed him back to health."

How déjà vu, I thought. I wondered if my grandfather had washed up on this very beach after his accident. Ancient history repeating itself.

"Did the princess marry Odysseus?" I asked, trying to suppress my sarcasm, but Danda just grabbed the basket and led the way down the escarpment.

At one time, the trail must have been a staircase, but it had eroded badly. Danda stopped at the bottom to wait for me, watching to see if I would fall and kill myself. I resorted to sliding on my butt, like a wuss.

"Odysseus did not marry the princess!" Danda shouted. "He had

45

his own family waiting in Ithaca, as you must know." She pointed southward. "For ten years they waited for his return."

"At least he turned up," I said.

Danda waited until I reached the bottom before she said, "It was the gods who prevented him from returning."

"They can do that?" I said.

"If you are worthy of their affection, oh yes."

"Are you saying that the gods were doing him a favour by shipwrecking him?"

"Of course," she said. "He was uncivilized; he fought for many gory years in the Trojan War. What wife wants such an animal in her home?"

"I'm surprised he didn't give up trying to get home after ten years of wandering the seas," I said.

"What else to live for?" Danda said. "We leave home so we can return better people. All stories are the same, I think."

"So the gods allowed him to go home after his shipwreck?"

"He had become human again," Danda said. She was looking out to sea.

I liked the story. It had the ring of truth about it, myth or not.

Danda pointed to a rowboat near the rocks at the mouth of the bay. I could make out two people.

"He should be resting, not fishing," she said. She looked concerned. "Instead, he goes out with Georgio. I told him, 'Jim, this is the time to heal yourself.' But what can you tell a man who escapes from hospital? Can you believe it? People are bothering him to return to work. Lawyers, writers, fans, that Oscar Hartmann! I am quite fed up." She took dead aim at me. "He should not be writing. Do you understand?"

No, as a matter of fact, I didn't understand. So many people getting their snot in a knot because my grandfather didn't do what he was told. But I just watched them rowing to shore.

The older man with the white bandage on his head, that had to be my grandfather. He was hanging onto the sides of the boat. From that distance his face resembled the head of a match, ready to burst into flame, and as they approached I saw that his beard was as red as his face. The whole package, his persona, his vibe made him look like he had been shipwrecked. And, obviously, the gods weren't finished with him yet, or they wouldn't have dropped me into his life to rock his boat even more.

Danda waded into the surf, waving like a goofy teenager. She met the boat and helped boost it onto the beach, while I stood unable to take my eyes off him. Which is why I hadn't recognized Georgio. He was shirtless, and I couldn't help shifting my gaze to his muscular back and tanned arms straining at the oars. After he beached the boat, he helped my grandfather, who was struggling in vain to rise to his feet.

"You should be resting at home, Jim." Danda scolded him affectionately.

"Canna rest all day," he said. The Scottish accent surprised me.

Georgio got behind "Uncle Jim" and lifted him to his feet, but still, Grandfather was teetering.

"A fine state of affairs this is," he grumbled.

"A fine state, Jim," Danda said, fists on hips, "when a man cannot recognize his own granddaughter."

"I know who she is," he snapped, finally looking at me. "I'm not so daft as all that." He smiled at me, nervously, almost guiltily.

I removed my cap, wishing I could have looked a bit more like Roxana, or that I knew how to greet him in Urdu or whatever language my grandmother spoke, because this was the moment that Maddy wanted to hear all about, when James Bearsden's past finally caught up with him.

With Georgio's help, he headed toward me, looming taller than I'd imagined him, his hand out to greet me.

"Well, well, well!" he said, suddenly all enthusiastic. "Welcome, welcome." I took his hand, and then he said "Roxana" in a quieter voice that made it seem like he was actually expecting me.

I could have cried, you know, because here's this very significant person shaking your hand, and officially you're supposed to hate him, but something's changed radically now that he's holding your hand.

Of course, you want a hug, but never mind, because you can actually feel the person through their hand. You can feel their heart. And he wouldn't take his eyes off me, still motoring on with the "well, well, well," and "Roxana, Roxana," like he was lost for words, which I totally understood because I hadn't said a word myself. Then, still holding my hand, he said, "When are you leaving? I mean, *arriving*! Goodness me. When did you *arrive, gerl*?"

He placed a hand on his head as if to blame his coma for the blunder.

"Calm down, Jim," Danda said. "Let go of her. You're still holding her hand, Jim." It was true, he was in a kind of daze. "Let her go, Jim!" she said.

"It's nice to finally meet you," I said, which brought him back to planet earth and made him let go, albeit reluctantly. He didn't want to let go of me. It was so weird.

The Apricot Courtyard

Georgio stayed behind to wash down the boat with buckets of water, while Danda and Jim and I headed up the trail toward the house. The island was right out of a picture book of Greek myths. Limestone rocks rose up behind the house, their sharp edges worn smooth over the centuries by wind and rain and goats and gods coming and going. With hardy shrubs flourishing miraculously in every cranny and crevice, the mini-mountain looked soft and friendly. It made no sense that a person living in such a beautiful place would consider ending it all.

"Now, Roxana, ye must stay as long as ye like," Grandfather said. "A week, ten days."

"Stay all summer," Danda said.

Grandfather shot her a dark look that had no effect whatsoever, because she added, "Of course, you will stay for the wedding. I will write your mother and ask her to come also."

When Danda said "your mother" Jim gave her a sharp look. She had no idea what she was doing inviting Maddy. Any conversation was going to be littered with landmines. So I said nothing.

As we walked, Grandfather kept repeating, "Roxana, Roxana, Roxana," as if he couldn't get enough of my name, which, of course, he hadn't had a chance to use for how many years? Thirty-five? I felt sorry for him. He bombarded me with questions, asking if I was planning to go to university, and what was I going to be when I grew up, all that predictable stuff.

"Calm down, Jim," Danda said. "You're running out of breath."

She took his arm as we approached the patio, turning to glower at me as if it was my fault he was running off at the mouth. I followed them under the bougainvillea-draped trellis, and then through a broad archway that led into a small courtyard with a fruit tree trained against one wall. Jim stopped short of the front door, breathing heavily and clutching his chest.

Help! He's going to croak!

Danda couldn't support him, so I offered a hand. But he was a big man and we were lucky to get him into the wicker chair beside the door. I knew it was serious because of the voodoo stare Danda gave me.

"I'm fine," he said, which, of course, he wasn't. He grabbed my arm as if he was slipping out of this world and said something that surprised me.

He said, "I'm sorry."

What? He was apologizing? Seriously, I thought they were his dying words.

"It couldna be helped," he said.

Danda looked puzzled, but kept fanning air into his face as those words echoed in my head, and suddenly all that garbage about what a bastard he was didn't compute. There were things Maddy wanted me to say to him before his lights went out, starting with *Why didn't you write?* and volumes more stuff that would have happily clobbered its way up the escape route of my big fat mouth. But it wouldn't come out. Suddenly I was, like, *What if he had an excuse? What if no one was to blame for what had happened so long ago?* When he let go of my arm, I stood up so he wouldn't see tears in my eyes, and I retreated through the archway to the shady patio, my heart pounding. I heard them shifting and shuffling into the house, their voices getting softer, and a door closing somewhere inside.

All I could think of was telling Maddy, so I sat on the patio step and examined my cellphone. It wouldn't open; the hinges were totalled. Then a goat decided the phone was lunch, but I managed to keep him away with one foot while I prized it open. Lo and behold, it actually lit up, but before I could check for a dial tone that damned goat gobbled it out of my hand. I smacked him on the snout and forced him to drop it, but now it was a mess of goat slobber and grit. Plus the battery went dead.

Georgio arrived with a bucket of fish and walked past me, heading into the house as if he lived there.

"Not so much noise," I said. "He's resting."

He stopped on the patio and looked at me as if he hadn't understood me, until it became clear that he just wanted to hang out with me. He was definitely hot, and without wearing anything trendy or pretentious—no jewellery, no tattoos, nothing, and wearing only black grimy shorts. But the fish smell was ruining the moment.

"Well, go on," I said.

"I am go to New York," he said, proudly, putting his bucket down.

"Good luck," I said, confident that he wouldn't recognize sarcasm if it bit him on his very sexy butt.

"Thank you," he said.

So I was right.

"You stay here, Afionas?" Georgio asked.

"Me stay here?" I said. "No, but better here than New York."

"No, no, better New York," he said. "I am chef in New York next year. My cousin has restaurant."

"Good for you," I said.

"You will come to my cousin's taverna, yes? I make for you pizza."

"I don't live in New York. But I suppose you deliver."

"Deliver? What is deliver?"

"It means you get in your car and drive the pizza to my house," I said.

"Okay! Yes, I bring to your house, then you will please come to *my* house."

To my surprise, I was beginning to find him charming, so when he headed through the archway into the entrance courtyard, I followed him. That's when I got my first good look at that fruit tree. An apricot tree. Its branches were splayed out like two open arms waiting to embrace someone. It was the only feature in that whitewashed courtyard, very delicate and filled with apricots. That was a good sign. An expertly pruned tree meant that at least my grandfather knew how to care for plants.

The door was open. It might have been recycled from an old shipwreck. I stepped into the house. I got the chills, and not only because it was cool inside those thick white walls. It felt like trespassing, so I stopped and knocked. Voices drifted out from a back room, just murmurs. So while Georgio took the fish into the kitchen, I did some snooping. A typewriter caught my eye. It sat on a desk by a window that looked onto the shady patio and the sea beyond. I thought about the typewriter ribbon in my purse and went over to investigate. A blank sheet of paper was rolled into the drum of the typewriter. The keys had dust on them and, sure enough, the typewriter ribbon was missing. Suddenly I felt useful, as if I possessed the missing piece of a puzzle.

I didn't think anyone used typewriters anymore. Unless, of course, you lived alone on an island without electricity. Come to think of it, there weren't any light fixtures anywhere. No electricity! How cool was that?

I spotted some apricots in a glass bowl and held one to my nose. So fresh and tangy. Everywhere in the house were books, books, books. They smelled a little musty, all stuffed tightly into their shelves and stacked on the floor like leftover bricks. Magazines too, and board games like Scrabble and chess. Taped to the wall by the kitchen were architectural drawings of a lighthouse. The walls were covered with photos, mostly black and white mementos of Jim sitting around in cafés. Oscar was in many of them, looking much younger.

I bit into the apricot. Juicy!

"How long you stay?" Georgio asked from the kitchen.

"Only a few days," I said.

"I take you to fish," Georgio announced, stepping into the living room. "You will like."

"You mean, *you* will like," I said.

"Yes, I will like, because I like you very much," he said. Coming from him, it sounded sweet.

I handed him the bowl. "Here, have an apricot," I said. "But I should warn you, Georgio, if you think I came to Corfu to fall in love..."

"Yes, Corfu is for fall in love," he said, biting into an apricot.

"Maybe," I said. "But I came here to fall *out* of love."

In fact, if there'd been a nunnery in town, I would have booked myself a room.

"Nothing to worry with Georgio," he said.

He extended his hand in friendship, but our hands were sticky with juice, and when I jokingly turned mine over so he could kiss it, he actually did.

Danda emerged from the bedroom to badger him, pointing to the bucket of fish in the kitchen. While they argued, I went to the bookcase and pulled down a book by James Penman, identical to the one that Mr. Moustaki had given me, but in English. *Alexander in Love* it was called. I hadn't noticed before, but the cover graphic was a large apricot. And something else—a little fruit sticker on the apricot said, "Made in Shangri-La."

Danda appeared just as I was dropping the book into my backpack.

"How is he?" I asked.

She seemed to have the weight of the world on her shoulders. "I told him about Gretchen," she said.

That struck me as both courageous and dangerous, but she was clearly in control around there, and she proved it by herding Georgio and me out of the house. So the three of us left, each of us chewing on apricots all the way down to the isthmus.

While Georgio returned to the boat to collect the rest of the catch, I couldn't help but notice Danda's routine with her apricot pit. After sucking the flesh off it, she cracked it open.

"Like an almond," she said, showing me the pale little nut inside.

"Very good for you, you know. It is said to cure cancer." I must have turned up my nose because she said, "Jim does not like them either. I tease him, 'How can you be a writer, if you do not search to the heart of things?'"

"I don't even eat apple peels," I confessed. The goat wasn't interested in my pit either, which told me a lot.

After handing Danda another fish, Georgio headed for the escarpment with his buckets, but Danda stopped me.

"You are right about the computers," she said, and I could tell that she'd been thinking it over. "We will need more than computers."

"I'll make a list," I said.

"It will cost a lot of money," she said, looking at me as if I was supposed to do something about it. "You and I will talk," she said, holding the fish at arm's length and giving me a kiss on the cheek. I hadn't expected that.

Georgio was waiting to help me up the escarpment.

We turned to the village through the herb fields, Georgio leading the way carrying buckets that slip-slopped their slimy brine over the sides. Following in the wake of that fish stink was more than I could bear, so I lagged behind in the scent of heavenly thyme until he stopped and waited for me to catch up.

"I like very much you come with me to fish," he said, sounding suspiciously like he was proposing a date, and I imagined being trapped in a hot boat with dead fish.

"I've never caught a fish," I said. "I'll be a jinx."

"I show you. Is easy."

"I've got a lot of reading to do. Grandfather's book."

"I know his book. You like I tell you?"

Georgio wasn't going to take no for an answer, not today, not tomorrow, not ever. And since I would be gone in three or four days, maybe there was no harm in it. It's not like I thought he wasn't attractive. And he was so uncomplicated that I could imagine my being pregnant might not even faze him. Not that I would ever tell him.

"Can you keep a secret?" I asked.

"I have many secrets," he said, his rib cage expanding as if that's where he had them locked away.

"Then you don't need to know mine," I said, having second thoughts.

"I am the best secret keeper," he said, and with such pride that I realized that they were other people's secrets he was talking about. I needed someone to confide my secret to. But Georgio?

I tried to imagine how Doug would react. To be honest, I couldn't. Then a more hideous vision presented itself—finding myself stuck with the Dooger forever. *Good God.* What if he actually wanted to marry me? *Eeyuk!* The thought was enough to turn me against this whole pregnancy thing.

Georgio set his buckets down so he could place both hands over his heart. "Uncle Jim tell many things to Georgio," he said. "Is safe in here."

Excuse me? My grandfather was entrusting secrets to Georgio? I wouldn't say I felt jealous exactly, but I certainly had a great big *hmmm* buzzing in my head.

"Since you know so much about Uncle Jim," I said, "isn't it true that he'd rather I weren't here, that I hadn't come?"

"Do not be angry with Jim."

"I'm not angry," I said. "I'm wondering if he's the one who's angry. Is he always so tense?"

Everything I said, Georgio had to add it up, syllable by syllable, so I spoke more slowly. "I want to hear what he has to say—about my mother."

"You come tomorrow, he like to talk."

"You didn't see what happened," I said. "He nearly fainted." Georgio didn't understand. "Fall over," I explained. It was definitely time to start speaking in special English. "Listen to me, Georgio. Jim's family—me, his granddaughter—not welcome here. You understand? I'm a ghost from the past. You know *ghost*? Dead but alive. His family is dead. Suddenly here I am, alive. Ta-da! Not good. Not good for getting married to Danda. No one in the village knew about his family."

"He tell to me about his family," he said. "His daughter, yes?"

"Yes, his daughter is my mother," I said. "Has he told you about her? Daughter is very angry at him."

"Jim tell everything."

"Tell everything to everybody?" I said.

"No. Tell me, only Georgio."

Okay, I was officially jealous. I had to believe him, because otherwise the village would have known about his family before now, instead of only recently getting their knickers in a twist. It proved that Georgio could keep a secret, even from Danda. I was impressed.

"So what does Jim say about my mother?" I asked, now curious as hell.

"She no like him."

"Just a minute, please—my grandfather told you that? That's not a secret, Georgio, that's a lie." It was so preposterous that I couldn't help but laugh.

"Jim, he tell me when we go fish. He is very sad sometime."

"*He* is sad? I think you've got that wrong, Georgio."

"Please?" he said.

I couldn't believe he was seriously blaming it on my mother. "Listen, Georgio, *he* ditched *her*."

"*Ditched?*"

"Ditched, yes. Split, ran away, bye-bye, *au revoir, hasta la vista*. A long time ago, okay? When my mother was a baby." Georgio was shaking his head as if I had it wrong. He picked up his buckets. "Yes, Georgio, your precious Uncle Jim gave her away. Jim gave the baby to his sister. The baby never saw him again."

"Uncle Jim is very sad she not write him a letter," he said, walking away. "She forgets her own father."

"She's never seen her father, don't you get it? What right does *he* have to be sad?"

He didn't stop, so I followed him like a shrew.

"Can we at least get the facts straight?" I shouted. "We never saw him, ever! I've never met him! So excuse me, don't think that *we* don't like *him*. Well, as a matter of fact—" wow, my anger was bringing me to tears "—as a matter of fact, Georgio, my mother hates him!"

I could easily have taken revenge on Georgio for the whole family catastrophe, but I caught myself and let him go. None of this was his fault. Not to mention that he must have known things that I wanted to know. Not to mention that he was trying to be my friend. I ran to catch up with him, but the crying wouldn't stop and I realized that, in my condition, I was a freakin' hormone factory. No way I was embarrassing myself in front of him, so I watched him go.

When I emerged from the lane where the whitewashed tree stood in the turnaround at the end of the road, Georgio had almost reached his father's taverna.

"Sorry, Georgio!" I yelled.

He spun around and yelled, "Fish tomorrow, yes?"

"Maybe!"

"Bravo!" he shouted.

6

Snooping

The Kalypso Taverna was so packed, I couldn't even get in the door. Yet no one seemed to be eating. So what was it, a meeting? If that's what you call a bunch of men yelling at each other.

"Roxy Hunter!" It was Mr. Moustaki waving at me from inside.

Damn, I'd forgotten to call him! He didn't look upset, but he definitely wanted me to join him. Thanks to his shouting my name, every eye in the place was fixed on me, so I backed away. But Mr. Moustaki came after me.

"I think I know what this is about," I said, looking in from the doorway. "I've blown my grandfather's cover by showing up here."

A short character with eyebrows like electrocuted caterpillars was slamming his hand on the table.

"That's the mayor," whispered Mr. Moustaki, "Kostas Doukas."

"Why is he yelling at the priest?" I asked.

"For bothering your grandfather," Moustaki said. "Most of the villagers want him to leave Jim alone."

"I know, he wants my grandfather to join the church," I whispered.

"Very important in Greece to be married in the Orthodox Church," Moustaki agreed. "But the villagers are asking the priest to make exception for Jim."

"Because he's ill?" I asked.

"Exactly, my dear. But the Father is not accepting this. He is upset with Jim because he kept his family a secret. Everyone is upset with him because of that. They are asking if he is still married. Maybe something else he is hiding. I'm telling you, my dear, in Afionas they don't like people to have secrets."

I thought of my own secret and wished I'd told somebody, anybody. It was gnawing at me, making me wonder how I'd ever imagined that being alone would help me decide what to do.

"They believe you must know something," Moustaki said.

"I don't know anything, honestly."

Mr. Moustaki pushed his way to the centre of the room and, with hands held high, quelled the storm. Although I didn't understand a word, I knew he was explaining that I was as ignorant as they were about Uncle Jim, and so, one by one, they settled down. Even Mayor Doukas stopped pounding the table and sat down.

Father Katadodis was the first to rise. People backed away to let him through, like the Red Sea parting before Moses. As he passed me, he paused and placed a hand on my head. I thought it was very nice, you know, to be touched in that way, like a blessing. I almost started crying.

After Father Katadodis had left, Mr. Moustaki took me by the arm and led me outside, steering me toward Stefanos Taverna. "What can a priest do? He is only doing his job. He is not wanting to get mixed up in politics—"

"What politics?" I asked.

"You don't know about the school?"

"Yes, Danda told me."

"A most generous wedding present," Moustaki said, shaking his head, "unless the wedding is too much trouble for your grandfather. To change religion is a big job. To change even the smallest habit is most difficult." As we passed under Stefanos' entrance arch, he added, "For some people, is easier to die than to change."

"That's why he tried to kill himself?"

Mr. Moustaki almost tripped. He clasped his hands in front of his face. "I did not say that, I did not mean it like that and, please, forget what Oscar Hartmann is telling you. He is so dramatic. Almost— how do you say it—like a drama queen."

Moustaki claimed the first table he reached, settling into a dubious looking chair with a seat made of rope. He looked exhausted, but there were questions I needed answered.

"Mr. Moustaki, how long have you known our phone number?"

"My dear, I am your grandfather's solicitor. Of course I know these things."

Which meant that my grandfather knew our phone number. How was I going to explain that to Maddy?

"My grandfather," I said, "is he actually going to fork over to build a school?"

"School building, playing field, football uniforms, everything," he said. "In ten years the village cannot raise the money for such a thing."

"Is he that rich?"

"I tell you a secret, Roxy," he said, motioning me close. "He does not know how much this can cost."

"So why—"

"That is why I came here today from Corfu town. To tell him. Again!" He raised his hands in frustration and then massaged his temples.

"*Yassou!* Dimitris!" It was an older man who headed our way with a glass on a tray. He was tall, with a mustache like the wings of a dove.

"Yassou, Stefanos!"

So this was Georgio's father. The men hugged, and then it was blah, blah, blah, all in Greek, of course. Dimitris took a breath, downed the drink in one go and then said, "Stefanos, this is Jim's granddaughter, Roxy."

He shook my hand politely, but I didn't quite trust the twinkle in his eye.

"Something for the young lady?" he asked.

"Do you have pizza?"

Stefanos looked at his watch as if to say, *Who eats at this hour?* Then he shouted over his shoulder, "Theo, Angelo, Georgio!"

"I'll tell Georgio myself," I said, standing up.

From the kitchen doorway, I looked in on a deep-fried hellhole over which a single dim bulb cast its greasy glow. Georgio was slicing and dicing something on the butcher's block while two cats crouched on the counter watching for flying tidbits. A woman's touch was nowhere to be seen. *Where was his mother?* I wondered. And why no ventilation? The New York Health Authority would close him down in a minute. Fishy vapours forced me back for fresh air.

"Hey, you!"

I glanced back to see Georgio coming toward me. The cats leaped off the counter and skidded across the greasy floor.

"You eat here?" he asked.

"I'll try one of your famous pizzas," I said.

"I make special job for you," he said.

"Cheese and tomatoes and basil, that's all. No meat, please. And thank you." I was glad to be back on speaking terms with him.

"You gonna love it."

He grabbed a ball of dough and danced it from one hand to the other.

"So, Georgio, you know all about my grandfather, yes?" He shrugged as he massaged the dough. "My grandfather is lucky," I said, "to have someone to tell his secrets to."

"Uncle Jim, he say I can write a book about him, when he is not in this world anymore."

"Better sharpen your pencils," I said, aware that my idioms were flying over his head. "Maybe I could help you write the book."

"Hey, you come fish with me. Uncle Jim, he like to tell stories when we fish."

The smell of fish, and now the talk of it, was making me sick. I had to get back to the patio and fresh air.

"Okay, fine, Georgio, I'll come fish. But don't expect me to eat any."

• • •

Mr. Moustaki was sitting alone, pensively swirling his drink, when I sat down. What a gentle fat face he had. The drink smelled like licorice.

"Can I taste it?" I asked.

"Goodness me, no," he said. "Your mother, she will fire me. She is sure to fire me if you don't phone her, my dear."

"About Grandfather..." I began. "He can write another book, can't he? To pay for the school."

"His next book..." said Dimitris, shifting in his seat. "Yes. If next one is success like the last one, okay, bravo! But where is it?"

"I don't know—where is it?"

"Not a word has he written for months. He is angry at me for reminding him, but what can I do? He is paying me to deal with his business matters. His agent in London is phoning me every week." He looked at his watch. "I must go see Jim now."

"He can't handle any more visitors today," I said. "He was a bit overwhelmed to see me."

"Oh dear. It is perhaps better to see him another time."

"I could mention it to him," I said.

"You're very kind," he said, touching my hand in gratitude, "but this is not your problem."

"Danda doesn't want him writing that book, does she? What's *her* problem?"

"Her problem is Jim, of course, when he becomes depressed."

"He gets depressed?"

"Writers, my dear," he said, shaking his head, "twice, they live their lives. The first time isn't bad enough. They return to the scene of the crime, to put it down for posterity. Why suffer only once? You can be twice as miserable the second time around."

It was funny the way he said it, yet all I could think of was how Grandfather had misinterpreted the "scene of the crime." If the past was depressing him, the least he could do was remember it accurately. Maddy had *not* rejected him! Quite the opposite.

Georgio arrived carrying a steaming platter of something hideous. However much he'd camouflaged it with batter, there were tentacles of some sort, chopped into rings and deep-fried, then sprinkled with parsley and served with yoghurt on the side. The whole thing made me gag, and Dimitris laughed as he filled his mouth. "All the more for me," he said.

But the appearance of my pizza returned my appetite. It was surprisingly good.

"You will phone your mother tonight?" Mr. Moustaki asked.

"I promise," I said.

He lifted his empty glass and shouted toward the kitchen. "Georgio! More *ouzo*!"

I phoned Maddy from the taverna at midnight as promised, and caught her as she was leaving for work.

"I finally met him," I said.

"Oh, my God! Are you all right?"

"Of course, Maddy, but *he* nearly passed out."

She burst into laughter. It was more like nervous laughter, crying twisted out of shape. So I moved my pregnancy to the end of the agenda when hopefully she'd have calmed down.

"So I haven't really *talked* to him," I said. "Barely a hello."

"Well, what else? What else?" I could hear her heart in her throat, and who could blame her?

"Nothing, really."

"Well, I'll tell you what else," she went on. "More incriminating evidence in Gretchen's drawers. Letters from him. Can you believe it? And a copy of his will. I suggest you be good to him because you aren't exactly forgotten in it. Unlike me."

"Seriously?"

"Seriously, my dear Roxana. He's got Roxana on the brain."

"I know, Maddy, I could've sworn he thought I was her. That's what he kept calling me, 'Roxana, Roxana, Roxana.'"

"I should never have called you that," she said.

"No!" I said. "I'm glad you did."

Both of us were now having a teary moment, so I couldn't ruin it by blowing her nervous system with rumours of suicide, or the money her father was going to lay out for a new school, or Georgio's twisted notion of who hated whom. And certainly nothing about me being pregnant. I described her father's house and the apricot tree and the goats and his latest book and his admirers and how quaint his life seemed. Her little sobs reminded me of the time I'd found her lying on the living room rug, and how I'd crept close to hear what she was whimpering about. "I don't have a heart," is what she was saying, over and over. I'd never heard anything so sad. And all because she'd blown an audition! "Mama, of course you have a heart," I told her, although from that day on I realized how vulnerable the human heart is, and swore to rely on it as little as possible.

"My father isn't going to die, is he?" she asked over the phone. She said it in such a way that I could hear that old prune of a heart coming to life.

I wanted to say, *Good for you, Maddy*.

Later, lying in bed, I realized how much I needed to hear those very same words from Maddy—after I told her that I was pregnant.

7

Interrogation

Xenia and the mayor were camped over coffee cups; they were the only ones in the dining room when I came down late for breakfast. It was a set-up, and not so subtle either. Mayor Doukas' eyebrows resembled barbed wire, and his questions were no less pointed: "What did your grandfather do after your grandmother died? Did he marry again?"

My answers couldn't have been more blunt: "Don't know. Don't have a clue. Your guess is as good as mine."

It embarrassed me to sound so ignorant about my family.

The mayor wanted me to help him find out the truth. I suggested that Danda might be able to get better information out of my grandfather than I could, but I agreed to ask him some hard questions.

"What else am I in Greece for anyway?" I said, with resignation.

"*Efharisto*," Kostas said, taking my hand across the table. "Thank you."

"That was not my idea," Xenia said, after Mayor Doukas had left. "Everyone in Afionas has a different idea about Jim since you have arrived."

But nobody seems to care that he might die of a heart attack, I thought, *just by my knocking on his door again.*

• • •

On my way to the peninsula, I had just passed the tree at the turnaround when I ran into three girls, probably tourists, coming up the lane toward me, all chattering in Italian about "*il Signore* Penman."

"How is Mr. Penman this morning?" I asked. *He must be feeling better*, I thought, *if he's throwing parties for his fans.*

"He is so nice man," one of the girls said, and they laughed their heads off. I realized why Danda wanted to ban visitors from Jim's place.

I reached the top of the escarpment and looked across the isthmus to the rocks beyond, where my grandfather's house stood shimmering in the heat. From that distance, I could hear every little chink and chomp from that gobble of goats grazing among the rocks. Then I heard a distant thunk, and saw Georgio's boat at the mouth of the bay, and Georgio in the water heaving some glistening dead thing into the boat with a splunch. I waited until he submerged again before starting down the escarpment. Someone—I wonder who!—had installed a rope, fixed at the top by a metal spike pounded into the rock, so that a person could rappel safely down the steepest sections.

As I approached the house, I found myself stepping lightly to avoid the sound of crunching gravel—probably not the smartest idea, since surprising Grandpa at close range could be the very thing that finished him off. I'd have to walk on eggshells to avoid all those taboo subjects like Oscar and weddings, and especially his writing.

Once I reached the patio, I had no choice but to suck it up and march in there, but I didn't have to march far because that's where he was, on the patio, in the hammock. Asleep. He was only wearing a head bandage and a bleached floral sarong badly secured around his hips.

Now what? Wake him up? That might be the most dangerous thing of all, because an orange cat was snoozing on his chest. I stepped into the shade under the trellis and held still, watching the cat on Grandpa's hairy chest rise and fall with every breath. The wish-woosh of waves and the breeze through the bougainvillea were enough to send anyone into a coma.

I inched my way past him into the apricot courtyard. The branches of the tree looked remarkably like arms outstretched in welcome. It must have been trained that way. A welcoming courtyard—what a concept! When the cat scooted past me into the house, I checked to see if Jim had awoken, but he was still snoring.

The house was deliciously and sweetly smoky smelling. Grandpa's pipes were laid out on the coffee table along with his sketch pads and at least four pairs of reading glasses. You could see how he lived, chilling out on the cushioned bench beside the fireplace when he wasn't at his desk. There were two bedrooms, my grandfather's and another one containing a single bed, a writing desk, and walls hung with life rings from various ships: the *S.S. Princess Sophia, S.S. Mimar* and *S.S. Mwanza.* How ironic is that? He almost drowns and here he has a house full of lifesavers. One of the life rings was autographed by Oscar. Why was I not surprised? I found a basket full of *National Geographic*s and other outdoor mags. A cover story by James Penman caught my eye, then other stories by him, and also by Oscar Hartmann. Those two had been all over the world. On the desk sat a sewing machine, and behind the door hung a woman's dressing gown. *Hmmm.* I got it—Oscar used to live there—until Danda took over. I was glad she wasn't there while I snooped around the house, and if I wanted to interview Grandfather I needed to do it before she showed up.

I tiptoed back to the main room where, from the window by his desk, I could see Grandfather snoring in the hammock. I decided to risk taking a closer look at him.

Though he smelled a bit smoky, there was something fresh and wild about him, almost fragrant, like sun on skin. What kind of country was this that could make a grizzled old man smell like perfume? I pulled up a stool and studied the hairs on the end of his ruddy nose, and the wiggly red veins in the pouches under his eyes. Up close he didn't look so good. Between his eyebrows were worry lines that made ninety-degree angles with the ones running across his forehead. Other little nicks and scars all added up to a life gone by. Gone by without Maddy and me.

"Why didn't you write?" I whispered. "Or phone or something." The cat mewed against my leg, as if she was making excuses for him.

A notebook at his side piqued my curiosity. A familiar photograph was sticking out of it: a snapshot of me on my first day of school. I plucked it gently off the hammock and turned it over. In handwriting that looked suspiciously like Gretchen's was written, "Roxana." I opened the notebook to find photos of my mother when she was a girl. Then I looked up and saw Danda crossing the isthmus, heading this way.

Damn!

The book fell from my hands, the photos scattering like leaves. Grandfather snorted. I left the photos on the floor and scurried into the house where I watched through the window as Danda arrived. She bent over to kiss my grandfather on the forehead, and it was then that she saw those photos strewn across the floor. One by one she picked them up, her fiancé's secret family. She touched Jim's shoulder. He grunted, opened his eyes, and realized what she was holding.

"Oh, Lord," he mumbled.

"How could you keep this from me, Jim?" she said. She was going to cry for sure. She let the photos drop onto his chest and said, "What else are you hiding, Jim?"

There it was, finally. The question all Afionas was asking. *What are you hiding?* If he responded, I didn't hear, because Danda entered the house and found me by the window looking guilty as hell.

"Hello," she said, with a hand on her forehead, gauging her temperature, it seemed.

"Danda!" I said, feigning surprise. I sank into Grandfather's typewriter chair.

"I need a big favour, Roxy," she said. "Please, can you make Jim's lunch?"

"For you too?" I asked.

"I only need a cup of warm milk," she said, heading for the bedroom. "To put me to sleep."

"You're stressing out, aren't you?" I said. "I'm sorry. I'll heat the milk."

Even though she closed the bedroom door behind her, I had missed my chance to be alone with Grandfather. When I heard him enter and head for the bedroom, I thought I'd lost him for good, but he found the door locked and retreated to his desk. When I delivered Danda's hot milk, she unlocked the door to receive it, looking ghostly pale.

I joined Grandfather at his desk, wondering how to break the ice. He was taking a pill with a glass of water. I was embarrassed to be close to him, since he was half naked.

"Mr. Moustaki was asking for you," I said.

"Good Lord. He's here?"

"No, yesterday," I said.

"Thank God."

I decided not to bug him about publishers and deadlines and bank accounts.

"I suppose he drove you out here from the airport in that black hearse of his," he said.

"No, Oscar Hartmann brought me."

He glanced out the window, suddenly alert, as if he might see Oscar crossing the isthmus. Or was I imagining things? Then he was back to staring at the floor, his demeanor as dark as a power outage.

"Oscar saved your life, didn't he?" I said.

"What if I don't deserve savin'?" he said. He rose to his feet, then stopped, realizing he couldn't escape.

"Oscar says hello," I said.

"He's not still in the hospital, then?"

"He should be, if you ask me," I said.

He stood with his hands on the back of the chair, staring at his typewriter.

"I really like Mr. Hartmann," I said.

"It's my fault, ye know. Everything's my fault."

"That's what Maddy says."

He glanced at me, and started to put on a khaki shirt that had been hanging over the chair.

"She didn't come with ye," he said.

"Oh, no, she's busy," I said.

"Of course," he said, sitting down. "She must be very busy." I couldn't tell if he was being sarcastic. "She must have been very busy to avoid me all these years," he continued, bitterly.

There it was again, *her* fault. It was all I could do to remain courteous.

"Is she still acting?" he asked.

"Who told you that?"

"My sister, Gretchen, who else?"

Then it was true—Gretchen had been in touch with him.

"Yes, she's a great actress. And what do you mean, *she* avoided *you*?"

"She might've taken the time to write," he grumbled.

What was he saying? Why were we even having this conversation? How could he get it so upside down?

"But, why should she?" I asked, trying my hardest not to sound impolite. "Excuse me, *sir*, but you never wrote to her."

He watched me uneasily, as if I was the one being mysterious. I mean, he seemed to be Google-Earthing my brain, but seeing nothing he sat back and said, "Wouldn't ye have been a wee bit curious? If ye were in her shoes, I mean. No wondering after yer parents? None at all?"

"If you're asking *me*, sure, I've always wanted to know about my grandmother."

"Yes, well, I'm truly sorry," he said. He couldn't look at me, as if I had a blinding light shining out of my forehead. "Sit down, Roxana," he said.

I sat on the leather ottoman and waited for him to start. And waited. His hands were so tightly clasped together in front of him that his fingers were turning beet red.

"You don't have to look so guilty, Grandpa. It's not your fault that she died."

He looked at me curiously, then seemed to relax.

"How did you meet her?" I asked.

"In Edinburgh, aye," he said, the love so very obvious in his eyes.

"In Scotland?"

"Ye didn't know that?"

"No."

"Ye have the same eyes, Roxy—like two sapphires."

"Sapphires—hardly," I said. "But why did Grandmother Roxana have blue eyes, anyway? Indians don't usually have blue eyes, do they?"

"Ye mustn't make that mistake. Roxana's people were from the north, a mountain kingdom unto itself."

"You mean, Shangri-La," I said.

"If ye like. No army ever conquered them. Not even Alexander the Great. He and his men rather took to loving them, instead."

I supposed he meant *making love* to them, probably at the point of a spear. It did explain how Roxana's people came by their blue eyes. So I was part Greek. While I was getting in touch with the blood that flowed in my veins, Grandpa started to fidget with the typewriter.

"Why did Grandma go to Scotland?"

In his mind's eye, Grandfather was right back there, years ago. "She came to Edinburgh to study midwifery," he said.

"She came alone?"

"Nay, her father brought her, installed her in college, then returned home. She wanted to study medicine, ye know, but her father wouldna go fer it. They needed a midwife in the village, and soon."

"What was she like?" I asked. I was worried that the memories might be too much for him, so I reached out and touched his hand.

"She was born to bring happiness into people's lives," he said. For a split second a lovely little smile escaped his lips, but he caged it up again.

"Was it love at first sight?"

"Oh, aye. At least, from my end of the equation."

"Wasn't she crazy about you?"

"I'm afraid, Roxy, that she was very much in love with a chap back home."

"Oh no. Really?"

"A young army recruit. Then, one day, she received a letter explainin' that he'd failed to return from the war. Of course, she needed comforting. I wasn't tryin' to take advantage of her in her moment of weakness—ye mustn't think that. I'd have done anything to make her happy. Then one thing led to another, seein' as she was boarding with Gretchen—"

"She was?"

"Ye didn't know that?"

"No."

He seemed surprised that I knew nothing, so I was glad to have established the all-important fact that I was absolutely clueless. I unleashed a barrage of questions. I wanted to know everything, including how he'd proposed.

"Proposed?" he said. "No! We simply rushed off to the preacher."

"No way! Without telling her parents?"

"Ye didn't know that?" He was definitely a little testy for some reason.

"How would I know that?" I asked.

I watched him pop another pill and chase it with a swallow of water.

"Her family wouldn't have approved of you?"

He took a long gulp, hoping to escape from my questions by drowning in a glass of water, but I was there waiting for him when he came up for air.

"Ye dunna understand her people, Roxy. Very traditional. No, they didna approve; I was a bloody disaster. Think about it, gerl."

He dusted the typewriter keys with a handkerchief, as if but for the lack of a ribbon and me bugging him, he might pour out his next novel. Then his hand clenched into a fist and he pounded the desk, making me jump.

"Didn't your mother tell you anything?" he growled.

Did she ever! I thought. All of it R-rated, including the speech

Maddy wanted me to make. Now was the time to earn my trip to Greece. And I might have, had Danda not been in the next room, probably listening to every word, and had Grandfather not slammed his hand down a second time, knocking over his water glass. As he reached to stop it from rolling off the desk, his chest hit the typewriter at the same instant that the glass shattered on the tile floor. One of his shirt buttons got snagged in that old keyboard and he couldn't free himself, couldn't sit upright without ripping his shirt.

"How could Maddy tell me anything?" I asked, trying to free him. "All we know is what Aunt Gretchen told us, which was basically zilch. I'm sorry, Grandfather, but your sister wasn't exactly our favourite person in the world."

"Mine neither," he said.

"And still you left Maddy with her?"

"It's a long story," he said.

"I want to hear it," I said.

As I freed him from that mechanical dinosaur, he said, "Are ye sure yer mother never said a word?"

"Grandfather, please, how would she know anything? It's not like you wrote."

"But I did," he said.

"Didn't," I insisted.

Grandfather smacked his hand on the desk as he tried to get to his feet.

"Sit here till I get a broom," I said. "There's glass everywhere."

I hurried back with a broom to find him holding his head in his hands. Well, he deserved a headache for telling me that he'd written. Maybe he had, but did he put a stamp on it? Did he put it in the mailbox? Obviously not. As I swept up those lethal shards, Georgio came lumbering in with his bucket, making such a racket that he roused Danda from the bedroom. Suddenly it was like Grand Central Station.

"Why is water on the floor? And your shirt is ripped, Jim," she scolded. "And who is bleeding?"

Sure enough, Jim's foot was bleeding, completely unbeknownst to him in his altered state. Danda gave me the evil eye as she helped him back into the chair, then ushered me into the kitchen.

"You don't come here if you are not taking care of him," she whispered angrily. "And keeping him away from that machine."

Wow, she looked worn out.

"*That machine* doesn't have a ribbon," I whispered back.

"I have taken it away," she said, "but I see that even an impotent typewriter can make him crazy."

She retrieved a first aid kit from the cupboard.

"We were only talking," I argued. "It's why I've come here, you know. And I don't have much time left."

When she checked her forehead for fever, I couldn't help but feel for her. I tried to relieve her of the Band-Aids, but she hung on to them.

"Yes, Roxy, you can do me a favour—my girls are expecting me for an English class at one o'clock, but I cannot make it. Can you tell them class is cancelled?"

Did I have a choice? Grandfather was finished for the day. Maybe finished with me for good.

"Sure," I said.

As Georgio and I left the house, he stopped in the courtyard to pluck apricots from the tree. Holding one in his mouth, he deposited a handful into my pack and handed one to me.

"They are good luck," he said.

"Come on, Georgio—you just made that up," I said.

He shrugged. "Okay, you are right. But me, I very much like this tree. Sometimes I talk to it."

"That's why it's so healthy," I said.

"Jim, he talk to it too."

"What does he say? Or is that one of your secrets?"

"He tell me, this tree is very patient."

"Yes, that's certainly a noble trait. We can learn a lot from plants."

"I am not so patient like that," Georgio said, biting into his apricot.

"Me neither," I said, taking a big sloppy bite out of mine.

We laughed.

As we headed for the isthmus, I had the feeling that Georgio and I were on the same wavelength. Two people can travel a long way on a tank full of simpatico. But I only had two days left.

8

Tattooed on My Heart

We chewed on those apricots as we crossed the isthmus. When I attempted to crack the stone between my teeth as Danda had done, Georgio took it from me. I thought he was going to show me how, but instead he threw both our pits as far as he could into the bay.

"I no like," he said.

"I thought the pits were good for you."

"I no sick," he said.

Couldn't argue with that; he was the epitome of health. "Never sick, ever?" I asked.

With a hand over his heart, he said, "My heart, she is sick for you."

"Oh, please," I said, and laughed.

We were both laughing as we started up the escarpment. He remained behind me to make sure I didn't backslide, but he probably just wanted to touch me and, to be honest, the feeling was mutual. My feelings were definitely becoming less ambivalent under the influence of that intoxicating herb trail and the wind and the sun and the running to keep up with Georgio.

"Georgio!"

He turned around, the picture of innocence. "Yes, please?" he said.

I was toying with him, and I felt guilty knowing how much he liked me, and what he'd probably do for me if I only asked.

"What do you know about my grandmother?" I asked.

He turned immediately and resumed walking. Holding to his promise, the bastard. I respected that, but still... "Come on, Georgio! She's *my* grandmother, not yours." I kept close behind him. "She's not a secret, you know. She died giving birth, I know that. What's the big deal?"

"Roxana is in Jim's book," he said, without stopping.

"It's a book about soldiers!" I shouted. "Not grandmothers!"

"Alexander's bodyguard, he make baby with girl," he said.

"One of his soldiers knocks up a peasant girl?" I said. "Don't tell me that's supposed to be my grandmother."

He shrugged as he walked.

"Have you even read it?"

"Jim, he tell me."

"So you haven't read it."

It turned out that everything Georgio knew came from yakking with my grandfather while they fished. He didn't even know where the Himalayan Mountains were.

"The soldier, he sleep with girl in apricot orchard."

"If you say so," I said.

"Then a baby is growing inside her and he must, you know, pay her papa."

"Hold on a second," I said. "He thinks he can buy the girl? Like a donkey! Or a camel, or whatever they have up there?"

He set his buckets down and faced me, looking a bit hurt, and with a hand on his belly he said with the utmost sincerity, "She is having baby, yes?"

As if that explained everything.

"You mean, if I had a baby..." I said, "if I had a baby here inside me—and let's just say for the sake of argument that it was your baby—are you saying you have the right to buy me? Or that you would even *want* to buy me?"

"*Fisika!* I would like."

"Get real."

"Yes, I would like," he said. "How much?"

I couldn't believe my ears. "In case you haven't checked the calendar lately, Georgio, this isn't the Dark Ages."

I proceeded ahead of him, almost running, while Georgio kept on about the peasant girl, who had been promised in wedlock to another man.

I stopped. That rang a bell. I'd read about cultures in Asia that have a tradition of matching up girls with husbands when they're as young as six years old. Can you believe it? They end up marrying someone they probably have little or nothing in common with. Of course, I nearly wound up with Doug the Slug, so freedom of choice might not be all it's cracked up to be. But never mind.

"So Georgio, the pregnant peasant girl is supposed to be my grandmother? Is that it?"

I heard nothing more from Georgio.

Meanwhile, it was after one o'clock, and I was worried that Danda's students would be wondering where she was.

The kids groaned when I explained that Danda was ill, and they groaned louder when I told them the class was cancelled.

"Please, Miss, you teach us, please," a girl said.

"Me? Oh, I don't think so." I desperately needed a nap.

"You speak like on television," a girl said. "Very fast."

"Sorry," I said. "I willl sloowww dowwwn."

They laughed. Very infectious, I must admit.

"Your face very nice," another said.

I crossed my eyes—big mistake. They all went nuts.

"Let's paint pictures," I said. "Word pictures. Words that paint a picture. Of each other."

They all wanted to paint me, naturally, and I soon tired of

their many creative descriptions of my face. But when I saw how it loosened up their English, I began to help them get it right, first about my nose, which wasn't big anymore, but "strong." And my eyes weren't blue, they were "sapphires," of course. I fluffed up an imaginary head of hair and said, "Next year my hair will be like Miss Skandalidis'." That earned a giggle, so I gave them my best Danda impersonation, one fist on the hip, the other hand theatrically supporting some elevated thought, such as *modern girls of Greece*. The class squealed with delight.

"Settle down!" I said.

Had Danda walked in, I would have been mortified—especially because the lone boy in the class was mimicking the way I was mimicking their teacher. I approached him, and he ran for the door. Good. I shut the door after him so that I could commence damage control. To the front of the room I went and waited until they calmed down.

"I can see that you love Miss Skandalidis very much," I said. "You are very close to her heart."

If I finally had their rapt attention, it might have been because I was starting to mist up, standing there with my hand over my heart, feeling it thump.

"What is that, Miss?" a girl asked, pointing a finger at me—at my heart.

I looked down and saw my tattoo poking up from beneath the saggy neckline of my favourite old T-shirt. I easily slipped my shoulder out so they could see the tattoo over my heart. The girls craned their necks toward me in awe.

"Shangri-La," I said.

"What is this, please?" a girl asked.

"It's a place," I said. "A far away place that's very close to my heart. Like the Garden of Eden."

"*Paradheesos*," said one of the girls.

"That's it, yes," I said. "Paradise."

For a second, I thought I *was* in paradise, surrounded by those adorable kids. Then, I noticed the boy's face in the window. He ran when he saw me looking at him.

"Boys, who needs them?" I said.

The girls applauded me for that one.

That night, I stayed awake with Grandfather's book, reading it not so much as a novel but as a *National Geographic* article, as if it were painting a picture of my grandmother's life. The conversation with Georgio had made me more curious about those mountain people betrothing their young children. Grandfather had said that Roxana's people were very traditional—is that why the two of them had to elope? I couldn't sleep for wondering about it, and for puzzling over what Grandfather had said about Alexander's soldiers choosing love over war. That wasn't the Alexander I'd read about in school. Talk about an extreme makeover. But what can you expect when the author zips himself inside the hero's skin?

It was like a case of a wolf in lamb's clothing. Except they were both wolves.

Confessions

At seven o'clock came a knock on my door. Guess who?

"Fishing, okay? I am wait, no problem."

I lay under the covers, barely breathing. No one should be expected to face the world feeling so rotten. Furthermore, a dead fish was the last thing I wanted to see, ever.

Ten minutes later, Georgio was still there, scratching at my door.

"Not today, Georgio," I said, whispering through the crack in the door. "I've got stuff to do."

"Tomorrow, okay?" he asked.

I didn't have many tomorrows left. I couldn't believe the week was almost gone.

"Sure, Georgio." I said. "Thanks for asking."

"*Adio!*" he said.

I made it to the bathroom in time to throw up, then climbed back into bed feeling very pregnant. I wondered how women survived nine months of this. More to the point, what was I going to do about it? I had wanted to decide while I was away from Maddy. But how do you research something like motherhood? Google it? Interview happily married couples? See a shrink? At least see a doctor! Like, okay, the facts sure would help. Yes, I would see a doctor. Okay. I felt better already.

An hour later, I found Georgio helping Xenia fill saltshakers in her dining room. *He's stalking me, for God's sake!* And I didn't mind a bit. He made an amusing nuisance of himself all through my breakfast by doing impersonations of local characters like Mayor Doukas, complete with the table-thumping. He was very funny. When he finally left to go fishing, after inviting me one last time, I was on the verge of joining him.

"Tomorrow," he said.

"Sure," I said, "if I'm still here."

He opened his hands in a gesture of *What do you mean, if you're still here?* And with that same open-armed gesture, he seemed to be offering me *all this*, meaning Afionas, maybe all of Greece and, at the very least, all of him. As I watched him head for the peninsula with his buckets and spear, I imagined my girlfriends trampling each other to be first in his little boat.

I returned to my room and slept until noon. When I awoke I felt remarkably clear about one thing: I needed more time. I needed time to ease Grandfather into more stories about my grandmother. And okay, I guess Georgio was part of the equation too. Not that I'd mapped out a romantic strategy, but who knew what a few more days might bring? And, of course, there were those secrets of his, which, by rights, should have been mine.

I phoned Mr. Moustaki and asked him to cancel my flight.

"I'm ill," I said, which wasn't entirely a lie.

"What is the matter, my dear?"

"Throwing up," I said.

"Something you ate?"

Something inside me all right, I thought.

But I didn't set him straight.

The problem with spinning little webs of deceit is that innocent people get caught in them, like poor Xenia, who was obliged to bring lunch to my room on a tray. Moustaki had called her, of course. What did I expect?

"Xenia, do you know a doctor I can see?" I asked. "A woman doctor."

"Woman doctor?" she said, giving me a funny look. "My own doctor is very good, just nearby in Arillas. Fifteen minutes in taxi."

That was simple enough.

"Shall I make you an appointment?" she asked.

"Yes. Yes, please."

Xenia went downstairs to make the call. Big relief. Then, suddenly, a new anxiety—that the doctor would discover that I *wasn't* pregnant. This came right out of nowhere. *Do I actually want this baby?* It would be social suicide if I kept it, so why was I even considering it? It would probably ruin my life. Curses worked that way, no doubt, taking over your brain. Man, I hated all this bickering with myself, because the point of it all was a child, someone to love. I just didn't know how to handle it. That was the problem. Fine, great. Now what?

Xenia returned to my room to tell me that she'd made an appointment for five o'clock. I couldn't sit in my room all day asking, *Now what?* So I grabbed my pack and wandered away from the village. It became like a mantra as I walked—*Now what, now what?* I had to deal with it! Thank God I'd finished high school. That was a blessing. But it still didn't solve the question: *now what?* The doctor was sure to ask me.

At the first fork in the road, a sign pointed left to Arillas. The road undulated pleasantly downhill, so I took it. I was hours early, but I couldn't help it. I was a moth heading into the proverbial flame. I had to know. I *had* to know.

But I was pretty sure. Sure that I wouldn't be enjoying many more parties. Or boyfriends. Zero, in fact. There wouldn't be much sleep for a few years either, from what I'd heard. No more nights out with the girls. Nights in with baby was more like it. How would I even support a child? A monthly welfare cheque! Man, this was seriously bumming me out. I ate one of the apricots that were getting nicely ripe in the bottom of my pack.

The road sloped more sharply downhill. A few cars passed. Most people waved, and some even slowed to offer me a lift. But I waved them on, because I was no nearer to figuring out how I'd support myself without a career. No, no, no—I absolutely wouldn't let that happen. I would follow Oscar's suggestion and become a writer. Feed my little darling her puréed peas with one hand and type with the other. I could blog about being a single mom, attract a huge online fan base and rake in thousands of dollars from Google ads. A professional mom! Cool.

Well, kinda cool.

Or not.

No, pregnant teenagers do not rock. Babies, maybe. But seventeen-year-old mothers absolutely suck. Disgusted, I threw the apricot pit into an olive orchard.

I arrived in Arillas all too quickly. It was a real beach town and packed with tourists. I'd forgotten that people came to Greece to enjoy themselves, bringing their whole families with them. There were kids everywhere. And orange plastic sun beds under pink and green umbrellas, and hardly a woman who wasn't nearly naked and brown as a kiwi fruit. Pregnant women too, at least a half dozen of them, with everything hanging out. It was gross, but kind of liberating at the same time. Behind the beach, the town went about its everyday business.

I asked at a pharmacy for directions to Dr. Vassilakis', and in two minutes I found myself outside the clinic door. It wasn't even one o'clock. I looked in. No one in the waiting room. Just the nurse.

"Roxy Hunter," I said. She examined her schedule. "I'm early," I explained.

"Dr. Vassilakis is having lunch," she said.

"Dr. Vassilakis is finished lunch," came a disembodied voice, followed by the sound of footsteps on the stairs.

The doctor was a man. *Damn.* He waved me into his office. Nervous as hell, I pulled another apricot from my pack.

He wore a slim mustache, and a small Band-Aid on his cheek as if he'd cut himself shaving. A bit slouched, a bit disheveled; he looked more like a private eye. He pointed to my apricot.

"I know where you got that," he said.

I gave it to him, and he sniffed it as if he was some kind of fruit connoisseur.

"*Efharisto poli.* Thank you very much. Sit down, please, Miss..." he glanced at his computer, "Roxy Hunter, granddaughter of my good friend Jim. It is a pleasure to meet you. Now, what—"

"I think I'm pregnant," I blurted out.

He stared at me for a split second, then clapped his hands and, without another word, opened a drawer and produced a plastic container.

"Washroom on the left," he said, handing me the container. "Please, Miss Hunter, a urine sample."

So far, so good. My bladder was ready for the occasion. When I emerged with my specimen, Dr. Vassilakis rose from his desk and took the container into a back room. He returned a minute later holding the stick. He asked to hear all about my last period, when it had started and when I'd had sex, blah, blah, blah. Actually, he was so extremely cool about it that I began to hope that a physical exam wouldn't be called for.

"And what does Roxy Hunter want to do with her life?" he asked.

"Writer," I said, surprised by my own confidence. It was the first time I'd said it out loud.

"More is written about Greece than anywhere," he said, proudly. "I tell you why." He stood up. "Western civilization was born right here. Archeologists are still digging us up." He lifted a heavy medical textbook and looked underneath, as if artifacts could be found in his own office.

He started to plot an itinerary for me, my onward travels to ancient sites in Greece, starting with Saint Spyridon's tomb in Corfu town, but his nurse poked her nose in to tell him his next appointment had arrived.

"Please, Miss Hunter," he said, handing me a robe and showing me behind a curtain. "Please undress."

Damn. Here we go.

So there I was on the examination table with my feet in the stirrups, and him going on about some tomb I should visit, trying, I'm sure, to take my mind of what he was doing, but failing miserably. It was totally freaky.

"What are you looking for?" I asked.

"Ah! Checking for STDs."

"Seriously, I'm not that kind of girl," I said.

"I am one hundred percent certain of that," he said. "But since we don't know each other—hmm?—my duty obliges me to make these investigations. And I can see that you are in excellent condition."

Despite the bags under my eyes and a pimple jamboree on my forehead, he proclaimed me "healthy as a horse." Which was a good thing, because then he said, "Yes, my dear, you are quite pregnant."

I must have looked surprised or shocked, which I realize makes no sense, considering that I already knew.

"I can show you the little stick," he said.

"No, I'll take your word for—" My throat closed off as tears welled up. "Sorry," I said.

Crying, of all things, and after knowing for a week already. I hated myself for acting like such a wuss. He handed me a box of tissues.

"It is perfectly natural," he said. "Look where you are, in a doctor's office."

"Does that make it okay?"

"A patient comes in here to be examined, yes? And sometimes their soul becomes naked too."

"There should be a warning sign at the door," I said.

"Miss Hunter, you are absolutely right."

He began to type like a fiend on his computer, pretty much ignoring me, which was fine because I needed time to get a grip on the fact that I was definitely pregnant.

Roxy! What have you gotten yourself into?

"Now, Miss Hunter, I am obliged by my profession to ask you a few questions. Since you are not married—you are not married, are you?"

I shook my head.

"I must ask how you are feeling about being pregnant."

Where to start? Confused? Surely he could see that. About to cry? *Oh, my God, no.*

"Oh, hey, I'm cool with it," I said. What a lie.

"You seem to be a sensible young woman," he said.

"I don't know," I said. "Not really."

He wanted me to book an appointment for next week to talk about it again, and every few weeks after that for a checkup, as long as I was in Corfu. I said, "Sure," just to get out of there, because I was dying to tell someone.

Dr. Vassilakis gave me a free sample of skin lotion for my zits, perhaps in return for that big fat apricot that he began to eat as I was leaving.

"Delicious!" he said. "From Asia, that apricot tree. Did you know?"

I was dying to email my friends back home, but the only Internet cafe was packed. And furthermore, for the first time since I arrived in Greece, I was ravenous.

Tavernas were everywhere along the beachfront in Arillas. Without knowing exactly what I'd ordered, I wound up with a salad in front of me. It came in a bowl, with a slab of feta cheese on top and a garnish of seventeen (I counted them) tiny olives, jet black and tangy amongst juicy ruby tomatoes, cucumber, red onion and green pepper. It was delicious, but the waiter was a pain, the way he hovered around me. I wanted to kill him, but I settled for withholding his tip to pay for the phone call to my mother.

I bought a phone card and dialed Maddy. It was five in the morning in Vancouver. Maddy would be asleep for sure, but I sucked it up and let the phone ring.

"What?" She sounded perfectly awake.

"It's me. Are you still up?"

"Of course I'm up. The film's over budget. We're working all night. I'm sleeping in my makeup. I'm a wreck!"

I listened to her vent about how haggard she looked. The longer she went without sleep, the worse she looked, and the worse she looked the better the director liked it. We both laughed our heads off.

"Mom, listen. I'm pregnant."

One incredulous pause later, she said, "You can't be pregnant, sweetie, you just got there." When I didn't respond, she started to laugh. "You're funny. Pregnant! That's a good one. You just want me to say *Good for you*, right?" She quit laughing. "Right?"

"Wrong."

"Mr. Moustaki emails me every day. He would have told me."

"How would Mr. Moustaki know anything about *Doug*?" I asked.

"Doug? What do you mean, Doug? Not *our* Doug." I was familiar with that deceptive calm of hers, like the eye of a hurricane. It was just a matter of time before all hell broke loose. "Are you kidding me?" she said. "Are you kidding me! You're kidding me. Tell me you're kidding me."

"I wish I was."

"My God! Are you kidding me?"

"Can we move this conversation along?"

"You can move your sorry ass home. That's what's going to move! My God, I can't believe it. You knew when you left? Why didn't you tell me? You didn't even tell me!"

"Oh, by the way," I said, "when Grandmother was a child, was she ever betrothed, do you know? Betrothed to someone else?"

"What are you talking about? Quit trying to change the subject. What's betrothal got to do with anything? What in hell's going on there? Put Mr. Moustaki on the line."

"Oh, time's running out on my phone card! Goodbye, Maddy! I love you!"

I was bad. Sometimes I was very bad.

• • •

I hiked back to Afionas along the shoreline until a jutting headland forced me up steep trails that soon had me huffing and puffing. Telling Maddy, though, was a huge relief. I felt lighter. Seriously, everyone I knew was constipated with secrets. Oscar, for instance, sworn to keep closed as a clam about something or other. It was killing him, and I don't believe that it was just my imagination. And Georgio, his secrets didn't even belong to him. They were Uncle Jim's. Even Gretchen must have been infected with Jim's secrets, and look at how she ended up.

10

A Terrible Mistake

Georgio stood at the bottom of the escarpment, waiting for me to rappel down the rope and land in his arms. Clever. We were playing a little game called "Would I Get into His Boat or Not?" At that moment, he was probably winning. So I slid to a few feet above him and let him wait.

"I've been reading Jim's book!" I said.

"Is good, yes?"

"No offense, Georgio, but—bullies with big swords—it's a boy's book."

He laughed, as if he understood exactly what I'd said. It struck me as miraculous how well we were getting along, so I let gravity take me into his arms. I was surprised that he let go of me so quickly, but it was to point across the isthmus where Uncle Jim was coming down the trail from his house. While Georgio readied the boat, I met Grandfather halfway across the isthmus and relieved him of his flippers and water bottle.

"You're still here," he said. I detected a note of relief in his voice.

"I'm staying a bit longer," I said.

"Yer free to use the house," he said as he brushed past me, waving to Georgio. Obviously, Grandfather wasn't expecting me to join them.

He greeted Georgio with a handshake, all jive-ass and roughhouse, which irked me. Okay, I was jealous. I was expecting Georgio to announce that I was coming, but Jim was already knee-deep in the water, with one leg over the gunwale. I rushed to lend him a hand. His considerable weight grounded the boat, so I helped Georgio heave until it was floating again and my grandfather yelled, "All hands on deck!"

Georgio and I were left holding onto the stern.

"Roxy come with us, Jim, yes?" Georgio said.

"It's yer boat, son—ye do what ye want."

"Never mind," I told Georgio. "I'll see you later. Maybe."

"He who hesitates is lost," Jim said.

"Are you talking to me?" I asked.

"Yer grandmother wouldna missed the boat for anything."

In a heartbeat, I tossed my backpack aboard and followed it over the gunwale.

"Let's go fish!" Georgio shouted, and he heaved his weight behind the boat to propel it forward, then jumped in and took charge of the oars, pulling hard.

"*Oh, Danny Boy, the pipes, the pipes are calling...*"

My grandfather sang the entire song before we reached the mouth of the bay. If there's a sadder song in the world, I don't know it. It's about a guy who leaves home to go overseas. I doubt if Grandfather realized that his life story was echoing off the limestone cliffs.

Georgio waited for him to finish, then heaved the anchor overboard and jumped in after it. Treading water, he adjusted his facemask, waved to us, then dove and kicked. We watched him until he melted into the inky blue and the ripples ironed out into a silky sheet of water that reflected the sky. The silence was deafening.

"Can I ask you something?" I began.

"I suppose that's why you're here."

I hesitated, not wanting to bludgeon him with a barrage of touchy questions. "Why did you change your name to James Penman?"

"Jesus, you're not reading that book, are ye?"

"I'm trying," I said.

"Well, it's what you'd call a pen name."

"It certainly is," I said.

He looked embarrassed. Rightfully so.

"I suppose it makes it easier for a writer to invent things," he said.

"You mean, if you used your real name, you'd have to tell the truth?"

He began fumbling with the strap on his flippers. Apparently the truth was an uncomfortable topic.

"I think I know how you feel," I said, trying to sound sympathetic. "You wouldn't believe what a mess my life is."

"Don't be too hard on yerself, Roxy. We all have our failures, of one kind or another."

"You mean, like, as a father," I said.

He reacted like I'd parted his hair with a bullet. I swear it had just popped out of my mouth. I turned away and saw Georgio near the rocks, brandishing his spear on which he'd skewered a wriggling fish.

"I'm sure your mother has reason to be unhappy with me," he said.

"On a good day she's unhappy," I said. "You don't really want to know about her bad days."

"Ye be sure to tell her that her voodoo spells have found their mark."

"Well, Grandfather," I said, "you could have showed up once in a while, you know." I was treading as softly as I could.

"She could have answered my letters," he fired back.

"Letters? I never heard about any letters."

"Of course there were letters, fer goodness sake, gerl."

"You mean letters with stamps on them? Letters in the mail?"

"What other kind are there?"

"I swear, Grandfather, there were no letters."

He seemed sincerely surprised, but not as stunned as I was, so we both sat there silently baking in the sun.

"Well, what did you write about?" I asked.

He set the flipper down. "What does a father say?" he said. "Simple things. Isn't it the thought that counts? Staying in touch. A bit of extra money. A pressed leaf, funny stories, people I met, books I published. And, of course, many times, I asked her to come. To come here and live with me."

My brain pounded behind eyes that stung with sweat.

"What are you saying?" I said. "There *were* no letters."

"I wrote to you too, of course," he said.

"That's not true, Grandpa." The sun had gotten unbelievably hot. "I would have seen the letters, don't you think? If they were addressed to me?"

"You'll have to ask your mother."

"You think she's been lying to me?"

"Do you?"

My life flashed before my eyes, and it was not a pretty sight. "How many letters?" I asked.

He looked down at his hands, fingers fidgeting, or were they counting?

"Please, Grandfather, tell me you're lying," I said. "How many letters?"

"A person doesn't count these things," he growled. "You believe me, don't you?"

Nothing made any sense. I began to feel claustrophobic. I looked for Georgio, but he was nowhere to be seen, so I stripped to my bathing suit and jumped overboard.

I sank. Deep. As deep as I dared. But when the water turned icy I kicked hard and pulled myself to the surface and hung onto the oarlock while I caught my breath; anger pounded in my throat— something bad was about to happen. I could feel it, some furious tirade that I would undoubtedly regret, so I swam away from the boat. I saw Georgio swimming toward me with some many-tentacled thing on the end of his spear, but I couldn't deal with his cheery mood.

"I'm swimming back!" I shouted.

Grandfather rose unsteadily to his feet. "Are ye a swimmer, Roxy? Are ye a strong swimmer?"

I had the strength to kill someone, so I figured I could swim a few hundred metres. I heard Georgio shouting, which made me swim harder. But my mind wouldn't give up on that outrageous lie. It had to be a lie. But what if it wasn't? Was Maddy to blame?

That's insane!

I used that rage to swim like hell—until a searing pain stopped me cold. My arm and chest were on fire! I choked on a gallon of seawater and started sinking, still too far out to get a footing.

"Help!"

So, Roxy, is this how you escape your fate?

Suddenly my mind became very clear, very focused on reaching the beach. I wasn't half out of the water when I saw to my horror the gooey blue tentacles on my shoulder and abdomen. I swiped at them as I struggled in the surf, gasping for breath, then slipped on a rock, twisting my ankle. Dizzy with pain, I managed to crawl up the beach on all fours like a dog, my arms and legs shaking. Then I puked.

Even though I could barely stand on my wonky ankle, I dragged myself as fast as I could to Jim's house and lay down on the bed in the spare room, shivering and whimpering and wondering if anyone had ever died of a jellyfish sting.

I still hadn't stopped quivering when Grandfather entered the room and sat at my bedside. I lowered the blanket and showed him the welts. The worst one was on my stomach.

"Mercy," he said.

It looked exactly like a fresh scar, as if I'd been cut open, and I began shivering all the more, thinking that this was all a bad dream.

Grandfather fetched a medicinal stick that smelled strongly of ammonia. It almost made me gag. It stung at first, but soon it cooled and soothed my wounds long enough for me to sip some mint tea.

"Here, swallow this," he said, handing me a pill. "It's an antihistamine. It will prevent an allergic reaction."

Mainly what it did was plunge me into a deep sleep. I dreamt that I was giving birth—by myself. And the baby wouldn't come, wouldn't come, and I knew what was going to happen, just the way it had happened to my grandmother—a woman's worst nightmare—

and I cried for help, pleading for forgiveness—and then I awoke with a start.

What the heck was in that pill?

From there my dazed mind took off into crazy, disjointed nightmares. I dreamt that my jellyfish attack was a cosmic message. I mean, it looked like I had a Cesarean scar. Meaning that my baby had been delivered. While I was sleeping? Obviously, it was aliens who had abducted my unborn child. That's how it happens—I'd read about it. I totally bought into the hallucination, even reasoning with myself, thinking, *Why would aliens want my baby?* And the answer came back to me like a foghorn in the mist, an entire chorus of ancestors:

"We thought ye didn't want it."

In my dream, I was thinking, *This can't be real,* so I tried hard to think clearly. Is this what happens to a girl when her hormones go berserk? Or had I actually miscarried? Shouldn't I be bleeding? Suddenly I was rushing to the bathroom, the details of which will not pass my lips except to say that as I sat on the toilet, I virtually exploded. Then the cramps! My moans brought Grandfather to the bathroom door to see if I was all right, but I didn't know, didn't even have the courage to look because the smell of blood—

I woke up. I was in bed with sweat pouring off me. I'd been dreaming the whole thing, yet I could still smell it, all fishy. I burst into tears.

Without a doubt, that was the most squalid, undignified, inexplicable, revolting, helpless and miserable moment of my entire life. To make matters worse, Georgio walked in with a tray and sat at the foot of the bed. He held a steaming cup of something to his nose and inhaled the vapours. Meant for me, no doubt. I could smell it—as primal as a swamp at the dawn of time.

"Please, no," I said. "I'm sick."

"Danda says is good for you."

"Don't BS me, please, Georgio," I said.

"I promise, is medicine from Greek gods."

I tried it—hot and salty. Surprisingly, the first small sip raised my spirits. I kept sipping.

"What is it?" I asked.

"Fish soup," he said.

What could I say? It revived me. It was a miracle.

Waking again, hours later, I could think of nothing else but asking Maddy about those letters. Not only did Jim not have a cellphone, but he didn't allow them on his island. Mine was in my backpack, wherever that was. I wobbled to the bedroom doorway, from where I could hear Danda and Jim in the living room. She was still on his case about his secret family.

"Where did Dimitris get your daughter's phone number?" she asked.

"Yer guess is as good as mine," he sighed.

She took a different tack with a brand new tone of voice. "No, Jim, my darling. My guess is much better than yours because it isn't a guess—it's a fact. You can find anyone on the Internet in five minutes."

I knew where this clever speech was headed.

"Have you heard of the Internet, Jim?"

"Aye, ye know I have," he grumbled. "No need to be patronizin' me."

"The new school should have broadband. And Wi-fi."

I could just imagine the calculator in his brain adding up how much more his promise to Danda was going to cost him.

After that, Danda looked in on me with a message from Xenia that Mr. Moustaki had called. I had been expecting that.

"You will stay here tonight," Danda said.

It wasn't a question, but an order. I hated the prospect of spending the night ruminating over the letters.

"Are you okay, Danda?" I asked. "You look a little tired."

"It is from worrying too much," she said, as she rubbed her tummy. "I have seen the doctor." She pulled out a pink Pepto Bismol tablet and started chewing it. "He makes me do tests."

Hello? Was Danda pregnant too? No wonder she was so moody. *Oh, my God!*

"Have you got an extra tablet?" I asked.

I wanted so much to confide in her. But what if word got out? What's more, I still hadn't decided what to do about the baby.

After sunset, once Jim and Danda had abandoned their Scrabble game and retired to bed, I considered taking a painkiller but felt sick at the thought of another pill. I was tired of feeling sick, and sick of being tired. Soon, the woosh-woosh of waves began to reassure me, and I imagined that the world might, after all, have a beating heart. And if not a heart, then perhaps an intelligence of some kind. A purpose. Some solid ground to stand on. Wouldn't that be nice, after seventeen years of living in a leaky boat. That's what it felt like, with no family standing by to rescue Maddy and me.

When I awoke in the night, those letters were heavy on my mind. Those supposed letters! *Was he lying about them?* My blood began to boil, turning the welts on my body into rivers of lava. What if Maddy had ripped the letters up? Had being abandoned turned her psycho? Or was it all a postal error? Or a wrong address? *Oh, my God.* Could it have been something that simple?

I limped into the living room. Moonlight streamed through the skylight. I remembered Maddy telling me once that Aunt Gretchen had never held her. Can you imagine never being hugged? It made me ill. Everything was making me ill.

I lay on the fireplace divan, my mind becoming an increasingly dangerous cage of monkeys. I got up and sat at Grandfather's desk. Big mistake. Those monkeys in my mind were hammering away on old typewriters. Pages were pouring out, stories of the way things might have been. It was driving me crazy. I stood up again. *Think of something calming, Roxy, something loving. Think of Grandmother Roxana Khan.*

I heard a noise in the apricot courtyard and slipped out the door to see the apricot tree with its arms open in the moonlight. It was as if that tree were my grandmother, holding out her arms to me. Hadn't Dr. Vassilakis said that it came from Asia? How weird is that? It was more than just a matter of feeling her presence; I could see her there, just as she had always been there for me. Then, suddenly, she ran off into the night.

"*Grandma!*" I screamed. "*Grandma! Come back! There's been a terrible mistake! You can come back!*"

I woke up with such a start that I hurt my neck. I was still lying on the divan. I hadn't moved an inch, hadn't entertained monkeys, hadn't chased ghosts, hadn't gone anywhere.

11

Not Just Another Pretty Fruit

*D*anda served breakfast in bed: fruit and rolls and cheese and tea, totally beyond the call of duty, and all because I mentioned that I had an elephant-sized headache to go with my fiery welts. I could appreciate what Grandfather saw in her.

"You eat like an elephant too," Danda scolded, as she brushed crumbs from the bed onto the floor.

"Actually, you should say, *You eat like a wolf*," I said, "or maybe a pig."

"Here in Corfu, like a goat," Danda said, looking out the window for a better view of Jim's little herd. "They eat anything. Be careful."

We could see Jim as he wandered behind the house holding a cup of coffee, and that's when she decided it was a good time to read me the riot act.

"If you stay here, please, you must keep him away from his desk. It is important."

"Important why?"

She glanced out the window again, then sat down on the bed. "This book is not good for him. This book—" She closed her eyes. "This book, I can tell you, it has almost killed him, Roxy."

"But it's only a story. How dangerous can it be?"

"The book makes him sad," she said. "I don't understand it, Roxy. Very sad."

"Can't he take something?" I asked.

"He doesn't believe in pills," she said.

"What the heck *does* he believe in?"

She picked up an apricot from the tray. "Apricots. He believes in apricots," she said, and took a bite out of it.

"I guess sad isn't such a horrible thing," I said. "People love sad novels. His book is sure to be a bestseller. Then you'll get your school."

She stood up, perfectly straight—I think she thought I was mocking her. "It is not a novel, Roxy," she said. "It is a memoir."

"You mean his life story?"

She picked up the breakfast tray. "Yes. As you can imagine, I will die to read it."

"You should say, *I'm* dying *to read it*."

"Fine, I am *dying*."

She looked like it too.

"You and me both," I said.

After Danda left, I listened to the faint rhythm of distant waves, interrupted only by occasional visits to my room by Grandfather with a cup of mint tea or a bowl of fish soup.

"I never imagined that I could be so useless," I told him.

"Not to worry," Jim said. "Things take time."

There would be no more discussion about those letters while I was recuperating, I decided. But how could I help but imagine what was in them?

In an effort to chase those damn letters out of my head, and to ignore the stings that were itching like the devil, I tried losing myself in Grandfather's novel. The story of the pregnant peasant girl had been another irritation for me, but at least it was an itch I could scratch by reading on.

In the story, Alexander's bodyguard marries the village girl. Then it seems that his fairy tale bride gets cold feet. She becomes fearful of leaving her valley to start a new life. She appeals to the village chief to protect her; and although there doesn't seem to be much he can do about it, a chief is obligated by tradition to listen to anyone who comes forward to argue in the girl's defence. The poor girl is convinced that leaving home will break her heart.

The sadness of the story exhausted me, and I fell asleep without turning out the light, but at two in the morning I woke to find the book still lying open on my chest. I returned to the chief's court, curious to see how—or if—the girl's family would defend her. Well, I found their testimony fascinating. All about a woman's role, her traditions, her obligations and expectations. About what sustains her, heart and soul—and they're not just talking about family. They're talking about apricots. Seriously. Apricots. In Shangri-La, they're not just another pretty fruit.

For young girls in that faraway valley, the sunny little apricot is the heart of their culture. They're experts at tending the trees. And harvesting, cooking and preserving the fruit. Right down to the glow on their faces, the apricot colours their entire lives. Daughters of Shangri-La who travel to the big cities in the south get fatally homesick, dying like fish out of water. I wondered if the stories were true because, if so, how had my grandmother managed living in Scotland, of all places? Was that why Grandfather had planted the apricot tree in the courtyard? As a memento of Roxana?

I swear, that apricot tree had been trying to speak to me since I had first laid eyes on it.

Despite feeling weak the next morning, I was desperate to get back to my own room at the taverna. I heard a fuss outside the window and saw a bevy of goats enthused about something up against the house. I leaned far enough out to see three kids feeding from a baby bottle that Jim was holding. He looked as proud as a grandparent while the kids, one at a time, sucked like crazy.

I dressed as quickly as my welts allowed, and joined him on the bench in the sun.

"They're starving," I said.

"They're goats," he said.

He handed me the bottle, and suddenly they were fighting over me. Me and my milk. I was feeding babies!

"I had no idea," I said.

"Well, now ye know," he said.

He beat the bullies away with his cane to ensure that the runt got his fair share. He sure did, slurping on the nipple at the rate of polishing off that bottle in less than a minute. Grandpa had a reserve bottle, and when it was drained, one of the goats licked my hand, then my leg where milk had spilled, and even then that rude animal kept searching for more on my leg until Jim pushed it away. We sat there in silence, watching the kids lick Jim's sandals where more drops had splashed. Eventually they strutted away, nudging each other and complaining in their throaty, grunting goat-speak until the childlike gleam in Grandfather's eyes vanished and a sadness set in.

Keep quiet, Roxy. "Things take time."

To my surprise, Jim mentioned the letters himself. "To think I might have died," he said, "not knowing those letters never made it."

He stood up and looked toward the water.

Shush, Roxy, or you'll ruin everything. Don't even smile. Keep your mouth shut. Let him come to you.

He lifted my backpack off a peg on the side of the house. I hadn't seen it there, drying in the sun.

"Here," he said. "Perfectly dry now."

I checked it over, inside and out.

"Where's my cellphone?" I asked.

"Georgio has it. I'm afraid he's tryin' to fix it."

"Does he know how?" I asked.

"I told him not to use too big a hammer," he said with a smile.

"Very funny, Grandpa."

In my pack, I found the little box that Oscar had entrusted me with. There would be no better time to give it to him, so while Danda wasn't in sight, I handed it over.

"What's this?" he asked.

"It's from Oscar."

Grandfather jammed the thing deep into his pocket without a word. "Did ye say he's still in hospital?" he asked.

"I said he *should* be," I corrected. "All twisted out of shape because of a broken rib, I think. He misses you."

"Aye," he said.

"Did he used to live here?" I asked.

Just then, Danda appeared around the corner of the house, standing there with one power fist planted firmly on her hip.

"I'll be heading back to the village," I said.

Danda headed toward us.

"Are ye well enough, Roxy?" Jim asked. "Danda, is Roxy well enough?"

"She's a Bearsden," Danda said, with grudging respect for whatever that meant.

"Well, I'll be off, then," I said. Spoken like a bad actress.

As I passed Danda, my sore ankle gave way and I stumbled. She reached out and grabbed my arm. I couldn't help but notice what a wreck she looked.

"Are you well enough, Roxy?"

"Are *you* well enough?" I asked. "Someone should be taking care of *you*."

"Thank you, Roxy," she said, proudly. "But I am a Skandalidis."

I could imagine a child by those two would be one tough little bambina.

"What letters?" Maddy demanded. She didn't know anything about any letters from her father. "Letters to me? What on earth is that man telling you?"

"That he invited you to come and live with him," I said.

"Listen up, you, this is starting to really annoy me—the pregnancy business and now this. Where's Mr. Moustaki?"

"Are you saying you know nothing about his letters?"

"I should have known you'd make things worse," she said.

"If they're worse, Maddy, it's nothing to do with me!"

"Well, *I'm* not there making them worse, am I?"

"Maybe you *should* be here," I said, "because I have a feeling your life is a bigger mess than you think it is."

"You're pregnant and you're worried about *my* life?"

I wasn't going to keep arguing with her in the middle of the taverna. Besides, Xenia was approaching me with her cellphone, mouthing the words *Dimitris Moustaki*.

"Gotta go, Maddy," I said.

"How many letters?" Maddy yelped.

"Didn't you say you found some letters in Gretchen's desk?"

"Letters to Gretchen, not to me."

"Maybe you need to search that desk again," I said.

Mr. Moustaki sounded depressed as hell about having to make my flight arrangements.

"I'm very sorry," he said.

"Don't feel you have to hurry," I said.

"On the contrary—my orders are to not let you out of my sight. Your mother thinks I have you on a leash."

"You'll be glad to get rid of me, I know," I said.

"Not at all, my dear," he said. "Not at all."

I actually believed him.

"Hey, Roxy!"

Georgio quit wiping down tables and jogged across the street to join me outside the Kalypso. I'd been watching him.

"How are you?" he asked.

"A lot better," I said. I hadn't noticed a glint of green in his eyes. "Thanks to you taking care of me the last few days."

"I like to take care of you," Georgio said.

"You mean, *liked*," I said. "It's the past tense—you *liked* to take care of me. I'm okay now."

"Yes, I like to take care of you."

"No, Georgio, you should use the past tense. Otherwise you're implying the future. And trust me, you don't want anything to do with me in the future tense." He looked confused, so I reached out and squeezed his hand. "You did an especially good job of making me eat that fish soup."

"I have more," he said. "Is cooking now. Come, please."

"What's cooking with my phone?" I asked.

"You will be angry," he said, looking sheepish.

"What? You made it even worse?"

"No, I fix. But now is lost. Jim is looking everywhere for where it is."

I took the pen from his shirt pocket and wrote my phone number on the inside of his wrist. "It's simple," I said. "Dial this number. Jim listens for it to ring, understand? He will hear it ring, yes? Bingo, we've found it."

I still hadn't let go of his hand when we heard his brothers shouting for him. Before he ran off, I added a little heart below my phone number. Upside down, it looked like a teardrop. I would be such a very long way away by the time it rubbed off.

And why exactly was I leaving? To get an abortion? Abortion was an option, yes, fine, but I hadn't decided yet, had I? That was the problem; I hadn't decided. And with everything going on with my grandfather, it was getting harder to make a choice. I thought seriously of visiting the doctor again, because he was the only one with whom I could talk about it openly.

I felt brave enough to risk my sore ankle on a short walk along a grassy path to the olive grove that descended in terraces all the way to the sea. I trekked down a trail of white stones to the first small terrace, from where I had a view to the sea below. The water shone like a slab of steel. No wonder Grandfather had chosen to live in Greece, especially after losing his wife. It would have been difficult for him to raise a child on his own.

I sat on soft ground against a stone retaining wall in the mottled light, closed my eyes and instantly felt a million miles away from my life with Maddy. It wasn't as if I didn't love her a lot. I did. She really had tried her best. I recalled one time we went to the beach—I must have been eight or nine years old. We made camp against a log to eat our french fries and mayonnaise, and before I knew it, Maddy started to sob. Way to ruin a picnic! I somehow knew it was about my father. She lay whimpering on the blanket while I continued to choke down those chips. In hindsight, I think she was blaming herself, which was unusual. I placed a hand on her hip so that she would know I was still there, and to be sure I said, "Mommy, I'm still here." She rolled over and said, "And I'll always, always, always be here for you, my darling," and she hugged me, crushing my ribs. I gave her the rest of the chips, and soon we were laughing, she through her tears, and that's when I realized what was important in life: sharing your love and whatever else you've got. Chips. Sadness. Hopes. Dreams. It didn't matter that little love-fests like that were rare; a person remembers. That little picnic of truth sustained me for years. But it wasn't until that moment on Corfu that I realized: Maddy herself had never been bolstered by that kind of parental love. Which pretty much decided it for me—she couldn't have got his letters.

So what had happened to them?

Assuming Jim had written them, had he not mailed them? Had Maddy somehow not received them? What if they were both telling the truth?

I'm not leaving Greece until I find out the truth, I thought. *I owe it to Maddy. And I owe it to the baby I'm carrying.*

12

Official Taster

"Roxy!"

Danda marched toward me along a pathway that disappeared behind the church. She must have been waiting all morning for me to appear in the street.

I was pretty sure I knew what this was about.

"Roxy!" She was wearing sunglasses. She meant business.

Father Katadodis appeared in the doorway of the church to see what the shouting was about while, over at Stefanos, one of Georgio's brothers stood at the entrance arch as if a public execution was about to take place.

"Roxy!" Danda shouted. "We need to speak!"

I hurried toward her, wanting to take this showdown off the main street. "What?" I asked.

She whipped off her glasses and presented me with Exhibit A.

"Jim has a typewriter ribbon," she said, her hand on her hip again. "You can please tell me where he got it. He says Oscar gave it to him."

"Well, it's true," I said.

"It is true that Jim is a sick man and should not be writing."

"It's also true that I deserve to know about my grandfather," I said, changing the subject.

"And you think I do not?"

She turned and marched off. I followed her up that narrow

lane, listening to her rant under her breath. We continued under overhanging pomegranate flowers, past olive oil barrels that were lined up against a long stone shed. She had the nerve to pull rank, as if being his granddaughter didn't mean anything.

"I think I'm at the head of the line, Danda."

"In line to do what?" she snapped. "To make him ride off in a boat alone again?"

"I've come all this way, and I don't have much time."

She grabbed my hand, pulled me to a doorway and motioned me inside. It was like being summoned to the principal's office. This had to be her home, a lovely renovated space with tile floors, rich blue stencil work on the walls and views over the sea. She lit a cigarette and offered me one.

"No, thanks," I said. "I quit."

Danda threw the pack onto a coffee table and it slid off the far edge. She didn't pick it up, a sure sign that she was having the worst kind of day.

"You shouldn't smoke," I said. I was horrified that she would jeopardize her baby's health, if she was pregnant.

"I will do what I want, thank you very much, and you will explain why you are trying to kill your grandfather."

"What are you talking about! I only want to know the truth. We don't know what happened back then."

She threw her disgusting cigarette into the fireplace and headed for the kitchen.

"Well, actually, I know about how Jim abandoned Maddy," I said, "but there's something else. He's hiding something. Somebody's hiding something!"

She returned with her pink bottle of Pepto Bismol and poured tablets into her hand. "I know he is hiding," she said. "From what I don't know."

"He and my mother can't even decide who abandoned who," I said. "How screwed up is that?"

"I am very glad you are telling me this, actually." She didn't look very glad about anything. She burped and crunched the tablets in her mouth. She was one sick puppy.

"Grandpa told me that he wrote to my mother for years," I said, "but she totally denies it. And I believe her, because no one in their right mind chooses to be the orphan from hell."

"What are you going to do?" She went back to the kitchen and opened the fridge door.

"Good question," I said. "Probably hang around and mess things up for you. Sorry, but our family has been a mess for ages."

She returned with two glasses brimming with something milky. Milk of magnesia settles nausea, I knew that. My hunch was right: she was probably pregnant.

She lifted her glass to me as a toast. "Yassou," she said. "To cleaning up messes."

I could barely hide my excitement. Both of us pregnant!

"So, Danda," I said, "you've got a lot on your plate." She sat down. "A lot," I repeated, "and something *in the oven* too, right?"

She glanced into the kitchen. "No, nothing in the oven," she said.

"Well, what's this, then?" I asked, holding up my glass. "It's a prescription for something, isn't it?"

"Dr. Vassilakis says to take it three times a day."

"I saw Dr. Vassilakis," I said, "and he gave me good news."

"I wish my news was good," she said.

"It's not?"

"Look at me, I am sick all the day."

"I know, but...it's for a good cause, isn't it?"

"I wish Dr. Vassilakis would tell me the cause." She rested her forehead on the palm of her hand.

"You're not...pregnant?"

Danda's face, even with her eyes open, went blank as a broom closet door.

"Excuse me?"

"You're not pregnant?" I asked.

Danda started to laugh. "Oh, no! I have parasites!"

Oh, my God. I hurried to the window to hide my embarrassment.

"In my intestines," she said.

She stood up to look at herself in a full-length mirror. "I am bloated with gas," she said. "Do I look pregnant, Roxy? That's terrible!"

"No, you don't," I said. "But I look like a complete idiot."

I could see through the window straight down the cliffs to the sea. I wanted to vanish off the face of the earth. Then I felt her hands on my shoulders.

"You are sweet, Roxy," she said.

"No, I'm not."

"You love children, which is wonderful. I have such a good report about you from my class. They are full of new words. They want you to come back again."

"We had fun," I said.

"I think I have been wrong about you," she said. There was a long pause, then she added, "Perhaps you can help him."

"Jim?"

"Talk to him."

"I've been trying to get him to talk to *me*."

"I understand," she said, her tone suddenly empathetic. "It is why you have come to Afionas. You can write down what he says, yes?" She sounded seriously excited about this idea.

I turned around. "You mean, be his secretary?"

"You listen carefully to what he is telling you, the whole mess, okay? Without arguing." She held up a finger as if that was the key. "Without arguing."

"That might be hard," I said.

"Yes, that is why it is absolutely the most important part. He must see that you are not upset. Whatever he tells you, you are just accepting it, okay? Eating it up."

"Like a goat," I said.

"Yes, like a wolf," she said. "He will see you swallowing his story and enjoying it—then how can he feel bad about it? He will tell you everything. You are devouring his story and it is not making you sick. Very important, you understand?"

"Like in ancient China where the emperor had an official taster."

"Except, you must eat the whole thing," Danda said. "Nothing left over for the emperor." She hugged me. "Nothing for him to chew on anymore," she said.

It felt good to be feeling good again, which made it the perfect moment to leave. As I headed for the door, she said, "And tell him that you are writing down his story into a computer. A computer! Do you understand?"

"Totally," I said.

I hurried along the pomegranate path in time to see Georgio emerging from the peninsula trail and heading for his father's taverna with his fish buckets, and five cats trailing behind him like a flock of disciples.

"Georgio!" I ran after him. "Did you find my phone?"

He shrugged and headed for the kitchen. "I'm hurry for lunch."

"Just tell me where it is."

His brothers were already in the kitchen hacking fish to bits and tossing them into a blackened cauldron of boiling water. A flying fishtail struck the light bulb in the ceiling before it fell into the pot. Not a chance I was putting a foot in that kitchen.

"*Barbouni!*" Georgio shouted, and pointed proudly to the witches' brew. "Fish with *limoni* and olive oil!"

The oldest brother juggled three knives, trying to impress me.

"Hey, Georgio!" I shouted. "My phone! Do you have it?"

He approached me slowly with that sheepish look again. "Please, ask Uncle Jim."

Another mystery, this time about a stupid phone. *Arrrgh.* I noticed a sweatband around his wrist to protect what I'd written. He must have seen me looking at it, because he raised his arm to his chest, wrist over his heart like some secret society salute. It was very nearly enough to convince me to confide in him about my baby.

"Hey, barbouni!" his brothers shouted.

"You'd better go help those barboons," I said.

• • •

Jim wasn't home. Weird. Not behind the house either. Weirder yet. Not even a goat. I ran down to the isthmus but the fishing dinghy was high and dry on the beach. Maybe he had a swimming spot behind the house where I hadn't yet explored. I climbed the rocks for a view of the other side of the island. Nothing, nobody, nada. So where was he? My heart started to pound.

I ran back to the house and checked the rooms again. He hadn't been at his typewriter. Had he gotten into a fight with Danda about her appropriating the ribbon? Looking through the window to the patio, I could see large sheets of paper lying on the hammock. They were the architectural drawings of a lighthouse that I'd seen around the house. A closer look showed a stubby gazebo-type structure sitting on a rocky summit. I stepped outside and searched the profile of the rocks. A helter-skelter network of goat trails led to the base of—well, you couldn't call it a mountain, more like a monolithic pile of rocks, really, but the highest ones were dramatic and blocked my view back toward the peninsula. He must have been up there somewhere with his lighthouse on the brain.

"Hellooo!"

Aside from my faint echo I heard a rock tinkling down, so I headed up those meandering ruts. The higher I hiked, the more there was to see until soon the whole spectacular coastline came into view. By the clatter of goat hooves on rocks, that's how I found him—not in the sun where I thought he'd be, but below the summit in the shade amongst piles of brick and a portable cement mixer. He was sitting in a plastic chair, feeding those goats again.

"You're not really building a lighthouse," I said, out of breath. "Don't you need electricity for that?"

"If Danda has her way, we'll have it, won't we?" he said, with a wry smile.

"Then you can finally get a computer," I said, moving closer.

"And all sorts of wireless crap, I suppose. What for?"

"You could email people," I said. "You could ask Maddy what happened to your letters. She swears she knows nothing about them."

He looked sincerely confused, even distressed.

I thought, *Okay, if he's pretending, he's a better actor than Maddy.* Then he said something I couldn't hear.

"What?" I asked.

"Gretchen." He mumbled it, as if I wasn't supposed to hear it, but loud enough that I would. He looked away.

"Gretchen?" I repeated.

His sister Gretchen, my mother's mother by default. The woman was depressed all the time and kept everything under lock and key, especially her bottle of whisky "for medicinal purposes." What a liar! And let's not forget how addicted she was to losing money at the casino.

"Excuse me. Did you say *Gretchen?*"

His sharp look said, *Don't make me say it again,* and he had to rise from his chair as if her name was a foul smell in the air that he might avoid. I never wanted to hear that name again either. Not a good word to say about anyone, that Gretchen, so if Maddy had nothing good to say about her father, you know why. Imagine her opinion of my tattoo. Imagine if she'd known about my condition! *You're going to hell in a hand basket, young lady!* Then she'd have carried on about the child who'd ruined her life, and how Jim had taken advantage of her in a moment of weakness. Her famous moment of weakness, in which she'd agreed to take care of Maddy temporarily. "That's all it was meant to be, a temporary arrangement," she used to say over and over. And how do you think that made Maddy feel? With her dying breath, I'm sure Gretchen blamed Maddy for being the death of her. It makes perfect Gretchen-sense, since Maddy had been the death of her real mother in childbirth.

So what *had* Gretchen done? Had she done something with the letters?

"Grandpa, you don't think that Gretchen—"

"Don't even go there," he said. "For God's sake."

But the movie was already playing in my mind—Gretchen intercepting letters. Too grotesque! All the scarier because I saw that the idea had infected his brain too.

"It's not really a lighthouse, ye know," he said, changing the subject. We both glanced up to the boulder above him, where he was looking.

"It's a federal offence, isn't it?" I said. "Intercepting the mail."

He pretended to be absorbed in his grandiose plans, but I could see he was devastated. "There'll be no beacon, ye understand," he said. "It's just a gazebo. I don't know—for writing purposes, I suppose."

It wasn't the best place to force the Gretchen issue, I thought. If something happened to him up there, Danda would never forgive me.

"So your stories will be the beacon," I said. "Like a guiding light?"

"Good Lord," he said. "Will people think that?"

"Well, Grandfather, you're up here in your lighthouse, and you being the brilliant author and all."

"How godawful!"

"Is it? I'm sorry," I said.

"Nay, yer absolutely right, gerl."

"No, really, you should build it. Honestly, if it works for you."

To prove what a great idea it was, I clambered onto the rock. It was steep, but no more difficult than climbing up a garage roof.

"Be careful!" he said.

The view from the top, back toward the Afionas peninsula, was enough to still the mind. The red tile roofs of the village topped the far crest of the ridge, and sandy beaches lined the coast. The sea shimmered in electric shades of green and blue. Far to the south, a rocky headland was crowned by what might have been a monastery. I could hear Grandpa at the base of the rock, mumbling.

"Are you talking to me!" I shouted down.

"Don't be mindin' me," he said.

To hear him better, I turned my back on the view and sat on my haunches, because now he was talking about money—British pounds.

"I might get a hundred pounds for a magazine article, if I was lucky. But, straightway, whatever I made, I gave it to her, ye understand, to care for Maddy. I hope ye believe me."

"I believe you. I believe you, Grandpa."

"Of course, I didn't mind payin', no, not at all. A man can live in a cardboard box if he has to."

"You didn't live in a cardboard box," I said. Then I remembered what Danda had said about digesting everything with a smile on my face.

"Perhaps not," he said, "but it had rats!"

"You lived with rats?" I inched my way back down the boulder as far as possible without slipping.

"Oh, aye, goodness me, Scotland's full of rats."

"Where was Gretchen, and Maddy?"

"We were in Edinburgh, of course. The three of us, little Matabhan and I, and my sister. You're not really in the mood for listenin' to more, are ye?"

Not much!

"So what happened next?" I asked.

"Well, my work was overseas, ye know, so I had no choice but to take a leave of absence. I couldna leave home. To keep the wolf from the door, I became a bartender. It was cash in the pocket at the end of the day—or should I say, from my pocket to Gretchen's purse, but that's neither here nor there. And at the same time I began writing my stories. Had 'em pilin' up in my head for years, I did. Even sold a few right away. Very encouragin', I must say, although it wasn't long before Gretchen was complainin' that I didn't earn enough, and perhaps she was right. I'm no sayin' she wasn't right, ye understand."

"She was trying her best for Maddy," I said.

"Aye. And so to keep her happy, I dusted off my engineering degree and set out once more for the colonies."

I crept down the rock as far as possible, because his voice was weakening. Had I slipped, I would have landed on him.

"Set out for where?" I asked.

"Africa."

The memory lit up his face. Like a light bulb. It was nice to see.

"On my return to Scotland," he continued, "miracle of bloody miracles, someone wanted to marry Gretchen—a man whose mind was set on immigrating to Canada. And off they went, little Maddy with them, on the understandin' that I would join them in Montreal. And I did. But there were no jobs for me. To make money, I began writing again. American magazines, I'm afraid. So there I was, making ever more frequent trips to New York and earning a decent living. But, my goodness, Roxy, talk about dog-eat-dog. I wasn't at all happy. By this time, Gretchen's man had seen the light—or should I say, seen the darkness. It did, ye know—a darkness hovered over that woman like a perpetual eclipse of the sun. Aye, he left her, I'm sorry to say. To escape his memory, she moved west to Vancouver. I suppose I should have joined them."

He stalled there, right at the point of abandoning Maddy. I feared that my saying anything would be like throwing him a lifeline, so I kept quiet.

"I'm guilty, of course," he continued, "by any measure of decency. Any court of law would have hung me from the highest gallows."

"Yes, but you needed to make money," I said, astonished to hear myself taking his side. I was only trying to I coax his spirits up again.

"That's right," he said.

"Vancouver is pretty and all," I said, "but it's no New York."

"Ye've got that right."

"But you didn't like New York."

"I didna take kindly to the New World. I longed to bring Maddy up in a place saturated with history, and I set out to find it. And I did. I did! Look around you!"

"Corfu," I said.

"The next thing you know, Gretchen won't hear of parting with Maddy. There we were on opposite sides of the world, but distance was no barrier to the transfer of money. Gretchen made sure I lived up to my monthly obligations, as she had every right to do. But the more I inquired about getting Maddy back, well, it's a funny thing. The more I asked, the less I heard from my sister."

The bitterness I'd harboured for years was dissolving with this story of his, transforming into tears of compassion for this poor man.

"I didn't know," I said.

I was on the verge of sliding down the rock and ruining everything, so I clung to that boulder like a leech.

"And when I did hear from her," he went on, "it was only to tell me how selfish I was for even thinking of disrupting her life by taking the child away from her. And in the same breath, how much more it was costing to raise a child, so 'please remit such and such an amount for such and such.' Fine and dandy, Maddy was a growing girl, so I gave up the writing business for a few summers to earn a steady income as a tour guide, if you can imagine that, bloody hell. And when I could tolerate it no more, I borrowed money and took up residence with the rats again. Actually, it was a quaint hotel in Corfu town. The writer, Lawrence Durrell, had called it home there for a spell, so why couldn't I? My God, gerl, Henry Miller had slept in the same bed! Can you imagine that? I was sleeping with literary giants! I was home, Roxy. And I wanted my child to come home too."

"So, like, Gretchen wouldn't give her up?" I said.

"I had to consider the child's best interest. You don't hear much of that these days, but it's the only question that matters. That's what it comes down to, doesn't it? A six-year-old starting school in one of the most promising countries in the world, or a life of uncertainty in a beatnik's garret? Enough said, I think."

His story made sense. Nobody, it seemed, had abandoned anybody. My whole philosophy of life, so suspicious and accusing, would have to be reconsidered. Dizzy, I started down the boulder on my derrière, braking my descent with heels and hands burning on hot rock, and ripping my shorts. If I didn't jump I was going to fall anyway.

"Having a child turns yer life upside down," he said, unaware that I was about to avalanche on top of him. "Until then ye've only heard about this thing called *unconditional love*. And as for that dreadful word *responsibility*, well, ye soon discover what a lovely side it has to it. Ye'll learn about it for yerself, soon enough, I'm sure, an attractive gerl like ye."

That settled it, I *had* to tell him. He'd essentially made my case for having the baby, for building a family. And he'd just bared his soul to me, so what was I waiting for?

"Come down, gerl, or you'll be falling on your head. There'll be two of us for the village to obsess over."

I let go and slid into his arms. Finally, our first hug, sort of. I smelled herbs and sunshine on his skin, and through his shirt I felt his physical strength, his fatherliness. I couldn't let go. Then he gave me a little pat on the back.

"I'm looking forward to having a baby," I said.

"Lord, no." He held me at arm's length. "You're far too young."

I should have known how he'd react.

"How old was Grandmother when she got pregnant?" I asked, knowing the answer perfectly well.

"Ye never mind that," he said, letting go of me.

"She was just my age, Grandpa," I said, eager to hear how he'd defend himself against such an obvious double standard. "You know, I'm almost eighteen."

"Ye don't understand, Roxy," he said. "Eighteen is an entirely different number where she came from. Marriage arrangements are made years in advance."

"Was Grandmother betrothed to someone else?" I asked. "To that soldier?"

He gave me that dark look of his, full of shame, like a tattoo on his forehead—the kind criminals got in Roman times. As he began to head downhill I could hear his invisible chains rattling.

"I'm sorry!" I shouted. "I'm not blaming you for anything. Anyway, I don't believe in that betrothal nonsense!" I ran after him. "Did she get homesick? Being away from her apricot orchards! It's in your book! Remember?"

I hated to let him go, but what could I do? So many unanswered questions. *Damn it!* I had the right to a few answers!

"Are you and Danda getting married?" I yelled. "It's not just me asking! It's the whole village! They want their new school!"

He raised his hands in surrender as he vanished around the corner of the house.

"And by the way!" I shouted. "Your school is going to need computers!"

The words echoed off the rocks.

I took my time coming down. What was wrong with that man? One minute we're hugging and the next he's running away at the mention of Grandmother.

I heard a goat bleating painfully. It didn't let up, so I tracked the noise to the far side of Jim's house where I peered around the corner. *What the bleep?* He was ramming his hand up the goat's behind. Half his arm had disappeared inside that poor animal, so of course it was objecting. And when Grandpa withdrew his arm, well, you've never heard such a rude barnyard noise, along with the goat's hind leg going into spasm and Jim trying to avoid it until he had freed his hand. A hand that held something.

My cellphone! It was ringing!

Grandfather opened it and held it close to his ear.

"Georgio? Is that ye, lad?" he asked.

I covered my mouth and ran for the isthmus. I would have thrown up—if I hadn't been laughing so hard.

"Mom, could Gretchen have stolen your mail?"

There was the longest pause. I mean, she could have hired an assassin by mail order in the time it took her to finally say something, except she didn't say anything.

"Maddy? Have you found something?"

The phone went dead. I didn't even get a chance to tell her Grandfather's story. No goodbye, nothing.

13

COURiER

I delayed my next visit to Grandfather until I'd spoken with Maddy
again. But I wanted to give her time to digest the possibility of
hijacked letters. Meanwhile, I was dreading Mr. Moustaki's phone
call about the flight arrangements that would whisk me away from
people I was getting to know and like, a lot. Including Georgio. He
was playing keep away with his brothers on the road between the
two tavernas. How to spend some quality time with him, that was
the question. I sat at a table outside Xenia's, keeping an eye on him
as I read more of that *Alexander* book.

Alexander's lieutenant—the father of the peasant girl's unborn child—
is dispatched to the battlefield and promptly gets himself killed. But
the story doesn't end there. After the child is born, Alexander claims
him. He wants to take the baby home to Macedonia as his own,
since Alexander is something less than a stud in bed, and his new
wife—an Afghan princess named Roxana—has gone many months
without becoming pregnant. So the reader can see why Alexander
might jump at the chance of an instant heir, and why the tribal chief
wouldn't object. Imagine, a boy from that valley becoming heir to
the most powerful throne in the world. But the chief can't sanction
the removal of the baby without hearing arguments from those who

object. So the court convenes again. These testimonies were the most interesting part of the book by far.

When the football bounced my way, I grabbed it. Finally, I had Georgio's attention.

"Want some help cleaning up your kitchen?" I asked. The brothers stared at me, dumbly. "This is a once-in-a-lifetime offer," I said.

"Hey, Georgio, she like you!" Angelo said.

"I'm mainly going to supervise," I said. "At least until I get used to the stink."

"Hey, Georgio, she no like our taverna," Theo said. "How you gonna marry her when she no can come in the kitchen?"

They roughed him up, all in fun, I'm sure, but Georgio didn't deserve to be humiliated in front of me.

"Fine! I'll clean it up myself," I said.

I grabbed an apron off the back of a chair and marched across the road toward their taverna. Such a disgusting place!

I was on Stefanos' patio washing the glassware in soapy water when an old black Mercedes rolled into the village. Mr. Moustaki! I had nowhere to run.

The car pulled up in front of Stefanos and, even before he emerged from the car, I could see how anxious he looked—even more than me. With a furtive glance across the street toward the Kalypso, he hurried through the entrance arbour into what he thought was the safety of Stefanos Taverna.

"Kali mera," I said.

He stopped in his tracks, then feigned delight at seeing me. Poor guy, he lowered himself into the first chair he reached.

"What's up?" I asked, apprehensively.

"My job, I detest it," he said.

"Don't lawyers make piles of money?"

"I will happily pick olives for the rest of my days rather than do what I must do today."

"Please, Mr. Moustaki, you have to tell my mother—tell her anything, that I'm still sick, that I'll come back next week, anything—but don't send me home right now." He held up a hand to quell my whining. "I know, I know, my mother will fire you—but so what?"

A sparkle, fleeting as a shooting star, lit up his eyes. Then, as if this was his big chance, Mr. Moustaki turned to me and opened his mouth, but nothing came out and he sank back into his chair.

"Anyway," he said, "I don't believe a word of it."

"A word of what?" I asked.

Where exactly is this going? I thought.

"Georgio promised me on the phone he didn't touch you," Moustaki said.

"Oh. That. Maddy told you, didn't she? I hope you didn't tell Georgio," I whispered.

"Heavens, no."

"He's innocent. I was pregnant when I arrived."

Moustaki couldn't look at me, just as I feared. Now I was one of the damned. He pulled folded sheets of paper from his suit pocket and shoved them across the table. It was a classic Maddy email, all CAPITALS and exc!amat!on marks and dramatic ultimatums and pregnancy factoids. Then he handed me an airline ticket, which revealed my departure date. Tomorrow!

"Georgio tells me you met one of our famous jellyfish," he said, cleverly changing the subject.

"Not tomorrow," I pleaded.

He deflected my complaints with his open palms as he said, "My dear, I am just the messenger. You must take it up with your mother."

I put on my best hangdog expression, but to no avail, because he changed the subject to jellyfish and his theory about how they're attracted to people with high-voltage brains.

"You will never find me in the water, my dear," he said. "Or outside during a lightning storm."

Georgio set a cup of black gooey coffee in front of Mr. Moustaki. He must have heard us talking about jellyfish because he said, "My father, never stung."

"Too busy putting the sting on women," Moustaki chuckled under his breath, and it was almost certain that Georgio had heard him.

When Georgio returned to the kitchen, I excused myself and got up.

"The ladies' room is just down that hallway," Moustaki said. "You will see what I mean about Stefanos."

I did see what he meant. Upon emerging from the bathroom, I saw photos covering the wall. Portraits signed LOVE BIBI, ALIKI, CONNIE or whatever. Almost a dozen different women.

"My father's girlfriends," Georgio said, appearing behind me.

I wondered, not for the first time, what had happened to his mother. Poor Georgio. I took his hand and squeezed it to lend him moral support, and when he didn't acknowledge me I planted a sympathetic kiss on his cheek. He wrapped his arm around my waist, drawing me closer and making my heart race. I swung around to face him so I could look into his eyes. I loved the pressure of Georgio up against my baby. Then I lifted my face to his and our lips met, just a touch. Okay, more than a touch. We were both too nervous to let it last long, but it did. It lasted and lasted with less apprehension every second. Eventually I had to pull away, though I didn't want to.

"I might have to go," I said. "I mean, leave for good. Tomorrow."

He looked heartbroken, though it must have happened many times before, tourists like me passing through his restaurant. I didn't want to think about it. I returned to Dimitris' table but didn't sit down. He had finished his coffee, and was looking at his watch. "It's getting on," he said. "Down to business."

"Please, Mr. Moustaki—"

"Not you, my dear," he said, standing up. "Your grandfather."

I accompanied him into the street where he wasted no time heading for the back end of town.

"I'll phone Maddy," I said. "You might have different orders by the time you get back."

"I wish you luck, my dear," he said.

123

"I wish you luck too," I said, keeping pace with him past the tree in the turnaround. "Jim is in a grumbly mood."

"Let's see how he grumbles when I tell him who might visit him next week," Moustaki said, shedding his suit jacket in the heat.

"Who?" I asked.

"His agent. From London." He kept up a no-nonsense pace along that narrow lane which deteriorated into crumbling walls and chicken coops. I had to run to keep up with him.

"Grandpa's already pretty wobbly," I said. "More pressure might not be a good idea."

"What can she do?" he asked. "She has pressure from the publisher in London. They want to see something."

"Something from his new book?"

"Yes, anything, a page!"

"Why the rush?" I asked.

Where those herb fields began, that's where I finally stopped, and so did Moustaki.

"But, my dear, they have been waiting patiently. And now the accident, goodness, they want to know if he still can type. Perhaps he cannot spell anymore."

"That's insulting," I said. Mr. Moustaki threw up his hands in agreement. "Why don't they leave him alone?" I asked.

He rubbed his thumb and forefinger together. "They won't pay him the advance until they see something," he said. "Can you blame them?"

"Don't tell Danda about this," I said. "She'll go ballistic."

He gave me that money-grubbing gesture again, as if that's all she cared about.

"No," I said. "She's really concerned for him. She thinks writing about his life makes him depressed."

"I'm sure it does," he said, sighing. "My memoirs would be a litany of all the things of which I am guilty."

"Jim's feeling guilty about something too."

"Who in this world is not guilty of *something*?" He raised his hands and walked on, shouting, "I plead guilty, your honour!"

It was funny, the way he kept waving his hands about, completely forgetting that I was no longer following him.

"It's a miracle we have not all set out in a storm!" he yelled. "Without a life jacket!"

I ran after him. "Does anybody know where my grandfather was going? In the boat, I mean—where was he going?"

"Away! To atone for his sins! I am thinking of making a reservation myself. On the next sailing!"

The pain in my ankle wouldn't let me keep up, but Moustaki stopped and waited for me.

"Is there room for me on that ship?" I asked.

"I am glad to see you have a conscience too, my dear."

"I came all the way to Greece to avoid telling my mother I was pregnant. You can't imagine my relief when I finally told her."

"Then you must help me to help your grandfather with his conscience."

"I'd love to, honestly, but how?"

"Set him to work," Moustaki said. "His book is a book of secrets, I know it. Everybody knows it. Help him to share, please, I beg of you."

He resumed walking.

"I've tried," I said. "He gets to a certain point and then shuts down like a power outage. Like a blackout. But I could try."

As we reached the top of the escarpment, I noticed Grandfather on the roof of his house.

"What he is doing?" Moustaki asked.

"I don't know, but if he sees me coming, he might jump."

Mr. Moustaki squinted into the hot breeze to see if I was right, because Grandfather was dangerously close to the edge of the roof.

"Jim!" Moustaki shouted.

He didn't see us until we'd crossed the isthmus and were hurrying up the trail. I could hear him cursing.

"Easy, Jim! No rush," Dimitris said, as he steadied the ladder.

"No rush? That's what I've been telling Danda, but apparently there's a panic." Once Jim stepped off the ladder, it was straight for the house without so much as a nod. "Well, I'm not putting solar panels on my roof, and that's that!" he shouted. "Ruins the whole look of the place. Where does she think we are? California? This is Greece!"

I should have trusted my hunch—it was too soon to be bothering him again.

We followed him onto the patio and through the apricot courtyard in time see the door slam in our faces.

"He is hoping a little rudeness might deter a lawyer," said Moustaki, "but he is sadly mistaken."

Mr. Moustaki didn't even knock; he just walked in and found Jim in the kitchen taking some medicine.

"I wouldn't have to bother you out here, Jim, if you'd get on the email."

Moustaki sat at Jim's typewriter and rubbed his hands together as if a show of enthusiasm might release a work genie.

"No ribbon," I whispered to him.

Moustaki took a close look, his sunny fat face clouding over like November. He pulled on the desk drawers but they were locked. When we heard a door close, Moustaki took up a position outside Jim's bedroom door.

"London is calling, Jim! New York and London! And now your old friend, Dimitris. Can you hear him?"

No answer.

"They want some pages, Jim. Anything. An outline, a list of chapters, that's all."

We listened. Nothing. I felt a twinge of compassion for Grandpa, probably lying in there with his head buried under a pillow. Moustaki knocked again.

"They don't know if you are even alive, Jim! Can I take your picture?"

Silence.

"It's fine for you and me to take our time. We are island people. But they live in a traffic jam, Jim. And everyone is honking at them. They send me here to honk at you. *Katalaveno?* Do you understand?"

Silence.

Dimitris threw up his hands in frustration and returned to the living room where he stood at the window.

"I own olive trees. Did I tell you, Miss Hunter? I dream of one day being known as Dimitris the Olive Farmer, with my very own olive oil label, but here I am wearing a suit—and ruining it!"

He brushed dust off his trousers.

"I now tell you *my* secret, my dear—I am a coward."

"Someday, you'll have your olives," I said.

I noticed a Scrabble game on the coffee table, with words like PERFIDY, ATONE, and KARMA on the board. "Some of these words...I've never heard of them," I said.

Mr. Moustaki snapped a photo of the board with his cellphone, and when he vanished into the bathroom, I looked in a dictionary. "Perfidy (noun): treachery, violation of faith, betrayal." I showed Dimitris when he returned.

"You can tell his publisher he can still spell, no problem," I said.

Mr. Moustaki waited another fifteen minutes in the hope that Jim would make an appearance. We loitered in the apricot courtyard while Dimitris carried on about how we must make him write, even one or two pages. It was our duty, yada yada yada. But I knew that Grandfather wasn't going to write about his life in indelible ink if he could barely chat to me about it. It was hopeless.

"Okay," I said, handing him back the airline ticket, "I'll do it. I'll make him write."

"You have three days, Miss Hunter. I will tell your mother, *three days*."

"A week," I said.

Mr. Moustaki further loosened his sagging tie and looked at his watch.

"Dear me. Your mother, after she fires me, she will sue me."

"Then we'll have time for some sightseeing," I said, hopefully.

"That's right—you haven't visited Saint Spyridon's tomb." His mood brightened, and he headed through the arch to the patio.

"But first she will have to find me in my olive trees!"

He turned to see if I was coming.

"I'm staying to make sure he doesn't jump off the roof," I said.

He snapped a photo of me picking an apricot, then repeated my marching orders. "Even one page."

With that, he was gone.

Hearing not a sound from Grandfather's room, I opened a copy of his novel and found where I'd left off. More testimonies from the peasants. The lengthy procedure begins to test Alexander's patience, but at the same time he's becoming increasingly curious about all this apricot worship, especially when it comes out that these mountain people are the longest living people on earth. The chief, for instance, is ninety-five and even he has elders who give him advice. Alexander wonders if that humble little fruit has something to do with their longevity. He asks the chief to explain how they're grown and grafted and nurtured and cultivated, because he is planning to take roots and cuttings home with him when he leaves.

I heard Grandfather moving about in his bedroom, so I set the book down and knocked on his door.

"It's only me," I called out.

"What is it? Is Moustaki still there?"

"He left. I'm just checking on you."

"Thank you."

Silence.

I knocked again. "I see you've created a wonderful life here..." I paused to let him respond but heard nothing, so I continued. "And I can appreciate that you must think I'm a ghost from the past." Dead silence. "No one would want their old family showing up, not when you're trying to start a new family with Danda."

He opened the door, startling me. "A new family?" he said, smiling curiously.

I'd forgotten that Danda wasn't actually pregnant.

"Well, she probably wants a child," I said. "Don't you?"

He laughed, the first time I'd actually seen him laugh, his old face wide and bright instead of long and serious. It was like breaking open a suit of medieval armour and finding a monkey inside.

"Danda canna have children." His iron visor clanked shut again as he moved past me into the living room.

"Are you serious?" I felt like the wind had been knocked out of me.

"Deliriously serious," he said.

It took me a minute to pump up my confidence to approximately the size of an apricot pit. Then I joined him in the living room where he was sitting at his desk, struggling to unlock a drawer.

"You could adopt," I said.

He grunted with contempt.

"Why not?" I asked.

"There'll be no more children."

"No more for *you*, maybe," I said.

"Ye be careful, gerl. I've seen ye with Georgio. He's not as innocent as ye think."

"Trust me, Grandfather. Georgio isn't going to get me pregnant."

"That's what they all say."

"I'm already pregnant."

He looked up, all squinty. "Say again, gerl?"

"I've been wanting to tell you. Some boy back home—who I'm not marrying, by the way."

"Ye canna be serious."

"You can ask Dr. Vassilakis."

"You're not keepin' it, are ye?"

"I'm not sure."

"Don't be daft."

He returned to his desk drawer, shaking his head, and pulled out reams of paper.

"Daft?"

"Do I have to explain? You should be out riding a bike, teasin' the boys, and gettin' yerself educated, above all. How are ye goin' to establish yerself, gerl, with a wee child holdin' ye back? Have ye thought about it? It makes no sense at all."

"I didn't exactly ask for this, you know," I said.

"No, but ye can undo it, and don't be wastin' yer time about it."

He slid a wad of pages into a large brown envelope. "I wish to God I'd undone a few things myself."

"No! That would mean I wouldn't be here."

He heaved a sigh and set the envelope on his knee. "I'm sorry, yer right, of course."

"And a family is totally natural. Children are completely natural."

"So are greed and deceit," he said. "And swarms of locusts. One hundred percent natural."

I was so angry at him. He was lumping my baby in with locusts! "That's terrible," I said, "talking that way about your *great-grandchild*."

That seemed to get his attention, but he looked away and changed the subject. "Ye can tell Moustaki I don't do outlines."

He stapled the envelope shut with a vicious line of rivets. He looked satisfied. "That should do it," he said as he handed it to me.

He opened his arms and cautiously wrapped them around me. Not exactly a bear hug, but a hug nonetheless. And this time it was he who wouldn't let go.

"Ye might catch that lawyer if ye hurry," he said. "It'll put him out of his misery. But ye'll have to hurry."

I did everything *but* hurry.

As I meandered back to the village, I imagined Moustaki well on his way to Corfu town. I stopped along the way to see if the envelope might be finessed open, but those staples were a virtual barbed wire fence. I reckoned I could easily slit the envelope with a knife. That's just it, though—I couldn't. *Stupid conscience!* But I was determined to read those pages, no matter what.

It began to bother me that Mr. Moustaki would have to return to Afionas to pick up the envelope. I supposed I might save him the trip by delivering it myself. There was a daily bus.

I arrived at Stefanos Taverna to see Georgio on the patio clearing away empty espresso cups. No black Mercedes in sight.

"Has Mr. Moustaki left?" I asked.

"Ten minutes," Georgio said.

"Oh, rats!" I was the worst actor ever. "I have something for him. From Jim."

"You catch him easy."

"No, no, Georgio. He's gone. It's too late."

Georgio shouted across the road to a taxi driver who was speaking to Xenia in the doorway of the Kalypso.

"Forget it, Georgio," I said. "I'll take the bus."

Catching up with Moustaki was the last thing I wanted. I chased after Georgio.

"I can't afford a taxi."

Even as he negotiated with the driver, Georgio pulled paper money from his pocket and handed it to me. Wild horses couldn't stop Georgio when he thought he was doing you a favour. The good news was that the driver had another fare, a young priest. The bad news was they were going all the way to Corfu town.

"Alekos is a good driver," Xenia said.

"We are catching Mr. Moustaki, no problem," Alekos said.

"But—but I'm not ready," I said.

"They are waiting for you," Georgio said.

"No, go, please. I'll take the bus."

"No bus on Sunday," Xenia said. "You should see Corfu town. Stay overnight. Go shopping. I show you where to find Mr. Moustaki. I will phone him. I give you a map." She rushed inside.

I had no choice, apparently. *Damn it!* I returned to my room to gather a few items I might need—like a pair of scissors. I took my time packing, to eliminate any chance of Alekos catching Mr. Moustaki.

Georgio held the door for me as I climbed in the back seat. Alekos started the car. He had no neck. Chest hair protruded from the top of his worn blue pullover, giving the impression that his head was sitting in a crow's nest.

"Something seriously stinks in here," I said, fanning the air away from my face.

"Fire in taxi," Georgio said. "Is good now."

Alekos told me the rest of the story once we were under way, about a cigarette butt that had found its way behind the ashtray and set the car's insulation on fire. "Big smoke," he said. He'd had no water, no can of Coke, nothing, no way of putting it out except by, as he put it, pissing into the hole in the dashboard. This was supposed to make me feel better? The young priest laughed and laughed. I bit deep into an apricot.

After ten minutes of swerving to avoid potholes on that winding road, Alekos' taxi broke down.

14

The Wedding Tree

Without a splutter or a gasp or a warning of any kind, the engine quit and we glided to a halt on a bend in the road. I wasn't sorry to escape from that stinkmobile.

A farmer happened along, whom Alekos seemed to know. He helped push the car backward off that dangerous curve and safely onto the shoulder of the road. Carburetor, that was the problem according to Alekos. Probably had piss in it. But the priest knew better and began disconnecting things. Together with the farmer, the three of them unscrewed hoses and nuts willy-nilly and tapped various parts with a hammer, each to prove their diagnosis was the correct one. I foresaw the sun setting on a heap of car parts by the side of the road.

I walked a short distance into the olive orchard to sit under a tree and examine that envelope, wishing to God that I had X-ray vision. It smelled musty, like everything else on Grandfather's desk. I was pretty sure I would break into that envelope the instant I could overcome my guilt. How simple it would be to rip it open and replace the pages in a different envelope. Who would know, besides me? And would Grandfather even have given it to me if it were so top secret? Maybe he *meant* for me to open it. After all, he hugged me, which might've been his way of granting me permission. I only had to look around to see that the gods were on my side—Alekos' taxi mysteriously dead, and me alone under an ancient olive tree.

Carpe diem. Seize the day. I cut it open.

How easy was that?

I slid out the wad of typed pages, and while flipping quickly through them, I heard a car approach. I looked up. A black Mercedes. It stopped. Mr. Moustaki! I stashed the pages in my pack and ran to meet him.

"You left an hour ago!" I said.

"My orchard is just here, nearby." He showed me an amber bottle on the seat beside him. "I have been testing my olive oil. But you, my dear, what are you doing here? Is that Alekos up the road?"

"We broke down."

I hadn't a clue what to say next. If I didn't hand over the envelope immediately, I would have to fabricate some bare-faced lie.

"Grandfather told me that if I left him alone—and if I came back in a couple days—that he would write something."

"Excellent. Well done. That's something, at least. Something to tell London. Thank you, Roxy, thank you."

"You're welcome."

"And so, my dear, where you are going?"

"Me? Where am *I* going?" I was stammering. "Alekos was going to town, so..." I knew I was digging myself into a worse hole. "...so I thought that you and I could visit that saint's tomb."

"Saint Spyridon. The patron saint of Corfu. Why, yes, excellent. Please, get in."

Phew!

When Mr. Moustaki started up the car, I was terrified that if he stopped to chat with Alekos, I would be found out. Well, of course he stopped. I crossed my fingers. And prayed to Saint Spyridon.

Mr. Moustaki got out of the car, opened his trunk and handed Alekos a tool box. That was it. Handshakes all around, and then we were off.

Phew, again.

"You can drop me at the Arcadian Hotel," I said. "Where I stayed before. You probably need to get back to work."

"Nonsense. You will stay at my place."

What did I expect? He was my chaperone. He wasn't going to let me out of his sight. I began to wish I was back in Alekos' smelly taxi, where at least I had my privacy. I needed time on my own.

Mr. Moustaki seemed to know only one speed: foot to the floor. He sang while he drove, songs about olives. I could see how much olives meant to him. Olives were his passion. Hearing him go on and on about them, it was obvious to me olives were his salvation. Like apricots were in Shangri-La.

"Is it true about apricots," I asked, "making you live to a hundred?"

"I tell you a secret, Roxy," he said, as he rounded a curve on the wrong side of the road. "To live good is better than to live long."

Attempting to break the land speed record may have been his idea of *good*, but it wasn't mine.

"I suppose Alexander the Great thought he'd live forever by eating apricots," I said. "Was that his plan?"

"Oh. You've been reading Jim's novel. Yes. In ancient times, life expectancy was very short," Dimitris said. "Alexander was already thirty-three years old and beginning to panic. No child! Good Lord! He has no time to waste."

"If he lives longer," I said, "he has time to have a kid of his own."

"It makes sense, yes?" Dimitris said. "If he eats enough apricots, he might live to be a hundred. That's two more lifetimes, think of it."

"So Alexander leaves with the baby *and* some apricot trees," I said.

"That is a happy ending, yes?" Moustaki said.

"Sure," I said, "if we ignore the mother who's left behind in Shangri-La to salvage what's left of her life."

Dimitris had no comeback for that.

"And I suppose Alexander just happened to drop off one of those apricot trees at Jim's house," I said, sarcastically.

He laughed, and when he saw that I wasn't kidding, he considered it for a second, then laughed again at the absurdity of such a thing.

• • •

Entering Corfu town, I had a case of déjà vu, except that I'd actually been along that road once before while riding in Oscar's car on the night I arrived. And there it was, the Oasis, the same creepy hotel that Oscar had rejected as crap. Moustaki pulled up and honked the horn.

"My place," he said. "You will please be my guest."

"You own the Oasis?" I asked.

"Oscar didn't tell you?"

Moustaki had business to attend to, so he left me in the care of Rebecca, a woman who emerged from the front door pushing a wheelchair on which three cats had caught a free ride. She was really something, this Rebecca, with her mascara and bangles and sandal straps laced to her knees. She took my pack and looked for more bags.

"Such a small luggage," she said.

That wheelchair was her luggage dolly—very clever. She ushered me to the reception desk, and as I signed in we heard another car honking.

"Oh, Oscar," she grumbled.

"Oscar Hartmann?" I asked.

"Coming from doctor just now," she said as she grabbed two keys off the board.

"He stays here?"

"Yes," she said with a sigh. "Here is key to your room. Room eight."

She handed me the key and showed me to the wrought iron elevator door. After I stepped into the tiny ornate cage, she reached in and pushed a button, then rushed to the front door, wheeling the chair in front of her. I waited behind the metal screen of the gate to see who would enter, and it was him, all right, still in khaki, but wow, he looked worse. He was out of breath from the few steps he'd taken to reach the front door. I reacted by closing the gate, which started the elevator with a clunk, and up I went, with a last glimpse of proud old Oscar refusing to sit in that wheelchair. I hadn't imagined that I'd see him again.

Reading Grandfather's manuscript was first on my agenda, but after that I would visit Oscar. He'd want to hear my news of Jim. When the elevator stopped, I stepped out and closed the gate, which caused it to clunk again, and down it went.

Room eight was next to the elevator, but my key wouldn't open it. I checked the brass number hanging on the ring. Room nine! *Maybe that's my room.* I knocked before unlocking it. No light switch that I could find in the gloom, so I crossed the room to open the shutters. Nice view, if you like the sight of grey roof tiles covered with pigeon crap. And more cats. This country had a weird love affair with cats. Two white ones leapt into the room, and that's when I saw the mess: books everywhere, and a khaki shirt hanging off the back of a chair. *Uh-oh.* I heard the elevator clunk and slam, and I hurried to the door. *Perfect timing.* I opened it and Oscar was right there.

"I'm so sorry," I said. "Rebecca gave me the wrong key. I'm supposed to be in room eight."

He waved off my apology and said, "Sit down, please, we must talk."

He made his way to the bed, but wouldn't sit until I'd done so first. Imagine that, waiting for me to sit when he himself could hardly stand. The only other chair was an oak monstrosity by the window and I plopped down in it. He took a pack of cigarettes from the pocket of a green robe lying on the bed.

"I am dying, so I smoke," he said. "You will excuse me?"

"Please, sir, don't mind me." I got to my feet again to be nearer to him. "Whatever makes you feel better," I said. "How are you?"

He touched the side of his chest. "A rib shticking here. Doctor says it is nothing broken."

Who was he kidding? He had a broken heart. I felt so sorry for him. He'd saved my grandfather's life and now he wasn't even welcome on Jim's island.

"The doctor finds nothing wrong with me," he said, "because I died already a month ago, but don't tell anyone." He chuckled. "It's a secret. I am a ghost."

He put the cigarette in his mouth, then he removed it again.

"How is my friend, Jim?" he asked. "Dimitris tells me that Jim thought you were his beloved Roxana, and then he passed out. Is it true?"

"Almost, yes—he almost fainted."

"Oh yes, I can imagine it. And then what happened? Please, you must tell me. What happened next?"

"You know, Mr. Hartmann, Jim had never seen me before."

"I know, I know. What happened next?"

"Well, considering everything, his moods and all his aches and pains, we've had some nice talks. Up to a point."

"Ah, the point, yes, I'm sure there is a point. I know that point very well."

"You do?" I said. "Can you tell me?"

He raised his hands to halt my question, and any further questions. "I say too much," he said.

I think he meant to stop *himself*, to stop himself from saying another word.

"No disrespect intended, Mr. Hartmann, but you're as bad as my grandfather. Secrets are killing both of you."

He set the cigarette between his lips so he could employ both hands to pull himself up and make his way unsteadily to the window. "I have made a promise," he said. "Remember?"

"Yes, you told me," I said. I was getting frustrated with all these secrets.

He stood at the window, lit the cigarette and inhaled with a vengeance, as if he could suck back everything he'd said to me. The glowing ash fell onto the back of his hand, the one that rested on the window sill, and what did he do? He watched it burn him. It must have been burning him, because he suddenly knocked it away. He gave me the impression of a man punishing himself. Maybe he was.

"He was writing about his life," he said. "Did you know that?"

"Yes, I know." And I could have proved it by pulling out the envelope and letting him read for himself. I was tempted.

"I must say," Oscar said, "Jim's life has been—you could even say mythic, if you are familiar with the story of Odysseus."

"His shipwreck, you mean."

"More than one shipwreck, goodness me."

"Danda blamed his troubles on the gods," I said.

"The gods?" Oscar scowled. "I thought she blamed me."

"No, not Jim's troubles—I mean Odysseus. Danda said it was the gods who shipwrecked Odysseus. They were making him civilized, so he was fit to return home."

"Where are the gods now?" Oscar said, looking around the room as if they should be right there. "Where!"

"You don't really believe in the gods, do you?"

"Of course," he said.

"You do? Then don't you see? They've sent you to help my grandfather."

He rubbed the back of his hand, as if the ash really *had* burned him.

"No one feels about Jim the way you do," I said. "Why are you protecting his secret?"

"For many years I have pushed your grandfather to make the right decision."

"Yeah, well, everybody's pushing him to make some kind of decision," I said. "Father Katadodis wants him to join the church, his publisher wants his freakin' book. I'm pushing him too, I'm afraid. To tell me the truth about his past."

"Your grandfather has a hunger hiding here," he said. He touched that poor heart of his again. "A hunger to make amends with his past."

"'The hungry heart leads home,'" I said, remembering the tombstone in the trunk of Oscar's car.

Oscar dropped his still-smoldering cigarette butt, and it bounced on the windowsill before it hit the floor. He stepped on it as he moved toward the heavy armchair, easing himself into it.

"I love that saying," I said.

"You can have it," he said. "My heart has not such a good appetite, these days." He closed his eyes and rested his head.

"It reminds me of my grandmother," I said.

Oscar opened one eye.

"I mean, it reminds me of Grandfather's book. The part where the chief is listening to the testimonies, remember? If the girl is taken away from her apricots, she's going to die of a hungry heart."

He opened his other eye and tried to sit up.

"My grandmother—I imagine she had a hungry heart too," I said. He was following every word I was saying. "Unless that *Alexander* book is all lies," I said. "It makes sense, though."

"How so?" he asked. "Please, please, go on."

"Well, girls who left the valley missed their apricots—I liked that part. And who can blame them, being from Shangri-La? Who would want to leave?"

Oscar was still listening, ready for more, but I'd run out of information.

"I'm going to visit my grandmother's birthplace one day," I said.

Oscar tried to stand. "I have something for you."

"What do you need?" I asked. "I'll get it."

He pointed to the closet, then relaxed again into the chair.

The closet was filled with boxes of old magazines. I sorted through them until I found what he wanted, a *National Geographic* from many years ago. He opened it to an article with photographs of those very women I'd been talking about. I couldn't believe it.

"Look!" I pointed to women drying their apricots on mats in the sun.

He nodded. "For your pilgrimage to Shangri-La," he said.

"You're giving it to me?"

"Yours, please. Everything you want to know about Kashmir."

He waved it away with one little gesture that dismissed the whole magazine collection, the entire room, his whole life, as if he wouldn't need another thing ever again. He made his way to the bed.

"Thank you," I said.

I had the urge to do something meaningful for poor old Oscar, to reciprocate somehow with a gift of my own. The manuscript seemed perfect, except I hadn't yet read it. But maybe this could work. It could feasibly release Oscar from that stupid oath of silence.

I handed the envelope to him.

"Something for you," I said. "It's on its way to Jim's publisher. They're in a big panic."

He felt the heft of it, as a cat at each of his elbows mewed encouragement. "You gave him the ribbon," he said.

I nodded. No harm in letting him believe he was responsible for Jim writing again. He dug into the envelope, pulled out the pages, flipped through them and began reading.

"I'll see you later," I said. He didn't seem to hear me. "Tomorrow," I said, "I'll pick up the envelope. I need it back. I've got to deliver it to Mr. Moustaki."

He didn't look up from the pages.

Alone in my room I thought, *Roxy, how stupid are you?* I'd given away the envelope! Why was I always putting other people's needs before my own? I couldn't believe it. That manuscript was my Holy Grail. I had to get it back. I had to read it before giving it to Mr. Moustaki.

Still, I had Oscar's magazine, which I devoured. All those photos of colourfully dressed Kashmiri women, jewellery galore, and I mean everywhere, around their necks, ankles, arms, ears, and on their heads. The article showed them wearing gold ear pendants that hung from silk threads. I imagined my grandmother being so outrageously beautiful. And their faces—they could have passed for Greeks, and, sure enough, the article spoke of their gene pool, a real mish-mash that included bloodlines from the soldiers in the army of Alexander the Great. The writer went on to say that when a woman married, she was often given a mature apricot tree as a wedding present. If that wasn't the oddest and most beautiful thing I'd ever heard!

I read it again. A tree as a gift. A gift for the bride. A gift that bears fruit for the bride who would bear fruit herself.

A wedding tree.

Naturally, the bride didn't dig up the fully-grown tree and haul it away. It stayed in the orchard, but only she was allowed to pick its fruit for as long as she lived.

I turned back to the first page of the article to see who had written

141

it, expecting the name James Bearsden, but no, there it was—Oscar Hartmann.

Too weird.

I lay on the bed with my head spinning. Could Oscar have possibly met Grandmother? I sat up again and checked the date on the magazine, then made a calculation. No, Roxana had died by then, two years earlier. Almost an amazing coincidence. I lay down again.

Mr. Moustaki's old hotel was a comic symphony of clanks, whirring, hissings, pigeon cooings and rattling window slats. Not a sound from Oscar's room, though, right next door. I wondered what he was reading, and whether it was the confession that Oscar was waiting for. I wasn't sure I would be able to wait for tomorrow.

I read in the magazine about *jardaloo*, recipes that used dried apricots, mostly in spicy lamb and chicken dishes. There were pictures of white apricot blooms in May and the fiery orange they turned in August, and I wanted so badly to see them for myself. I wondered if Jim's tree would do the same: burst into autumnal flames. That amazing tree had haunted me enough already, but now it was a *wedding tree*. Jim must have known that when he planted it. Must have. And planting it in the entrance courtyard, the welcoming courtyard, the place of honour. What a hugely romantic statement, the ultimate memento of a loved one. I was so impressed, but strangely disturbed at the same time.

Just a thought, but wouldn't the tree eventually become a liability? I mean, after all those years, and especially now that Jim was getting married to another woman. I put myself in his place, being in love and then losing his bride. Naturally, he'd want to remember her. So he created his own little virtual reality, Kashmiri style. Danda didn't know about Roxana, didn't get the connection with the tree, so how could it really cause Jim a problem?

On the other hand, believing that his daughter rejected him—that's something that could drive a person crazy. Not a single answer to any of his letters. I couldn't get my head around it.

How deranged would I get if my child ignored me to death?

Suspicious Fruit

I was showered and dressed when I heard voices through the wall from next door. Mr. Moustaki was there with Oscar. The walls must have been made of cardboard, because I could clearly hear Mr. Moustaki sounding surprised.

"Jim wrote this?"

Damn! He's seen the manuscript!

Oscar covered for me, thank goodness, telling Moustaki that he'd had it for weeks. "Roxy informed me," Oscar continued brilliantly, "that London should see this immediately."

Next, a knock on my door—and Mr. Moustaki standing there with the envelope.

"At last, my dear," he said. "I can show you the sights. Are you ready?"

But just then his cellphone rang, and he retreated into the hallway to talk. I could hear him answering detailed questions about James Bearsden.

He returned to my room, shaking his head. "I'm so sorry. Saint Spyridon's tomb will have to wait," he grumbled. "I have a meeting in Afionas this morning. Something has come up about Jim's documents. Nothing but damned documents. Imagine the inscription on my gravestone. *Here lies a man who signed bloody documents.*"

"You do more than that," I said.

"Yes, of course. I do meetings," he laughed. Then he looked anxiously at his watch.

"They're bugging my grandfather again?"

"When is Father Katadodis not bugging someone?"

"I see no harm in anyone trying to civilize my grandfather," I said.

"It is Danda who needs civilizing this morning," he said. "Kostas Doukas says she is ready to kill Katadodis."

"Why?" I asked.

"Over documents!" Moustaki said.

"What documents?"

Moustaki clammed up, only to say that he was late and that I should phone my mother, since she was furious with him for changing my ticket. But I saw it as a clever dodging of my question and followed him all the way to the elevator where he banged on the call button.

Big dilemma. Did I spend the day with Oscar to quiz him about what he'd read in the manuscript? Or did I stick with Moustaki to learn what he was covering up? As he shouted down the elevator shaft to Rebecca, his phone rang again and he turned his back and mumbled something about a death certificate. Even though the elevator had begun its whining ascent to the second floor, he was so impatient to escape that he waved goodbye and took the stairs.

Very strange.

I found Oscar's door ajar, and looked in. He was asleep in that massive armchair by the window, with those cats perched like gargoyles on the sill above him, purring so hypnotically that even a chronic insomniac would have been lulled into eternal dreamland.

"I'll be back this evening," I whispered, although I could have shouted, that's how dead to the world he seemed to be.

I caught Mr. Moustaki in the lobby where Rebecca was giving him hell, pointing at a crack in the door glass.

"I'm coming with you," I said. "If that's okay."

His normally smooth and shiny forehead went all crinkly with concern. "But, my dear, you haven't seen our museums yet. And our shops, goodness me, our shops! Ask Rebecca about the shops; they are full of wonderful linens and fine needlework and—"

"Dimitris. Take the girl with you," Rebecca scolded.

As we returned to Afionas, Corfu's olive trees became apricot orchards in my mind's eye. I saw Grandmother in every person working in the shade of those gnarled black boughs. When I reached Maddy on Mr. Moustaki's cellphone, I began to tell her what I'd learned about apricots in Kashmir—about fruit trees given as wedding presents—but she thought I was trying to change the subject.

"Love you, Mom," I said. "See you in a week! Break a leg!" Click.

"Most interesting to hear you speak of wedding trees," Moustaki said. He reached to the back seat to rummage in his briefcase. "Of course, these days, a bride prefers a BMW."

"Or a school full of computers," I said.

"That's it, exactly, my dear," he said, pulling out Grandfather's envelope. "For that very reason they are going to crucify Father Katadodis. He is interfering."

I took the envelope from him, so he could apply both hands to the steering wheel.

"Did Oscar show you this?" he asked.

I hoped it was the same envelope, which it was, and that it actually contained typewritten pages, which it did. That's when I noticed the title page—*The Wedding Tree*. A chill went right through me.

"You have read it, then?" he asked.

"No, sir, you have no idea how much I have *not* read this."

"That is quite remarkable," he said.

"You have no idea how remarkable."

"Myself, I haven't the time to read it," he said, "but perhaps you can look it over quickly and tell me what you think."

"Well, if you insist." I was already scanning the first page and thinking, *Pinch yourself, girl! You must be dreaming.*

"I just asked Hartmann for a review of these chapters," Dimitris went on, "but he evaded the question. Strange man. I like Oscar very much, you understand, but lately I must say he is acting strange."

The manuscript, I discovered, was mostly about his years of travelling in Asia and Africa, bringing "the miracle of electricity" to people in very remote regions. And about being treated as a king, and of turning down gifts of livestock and titles. But it was back home in Edinburgh where he fell in love with a girl from the most far-flung place of all. That's irony for you.

When he wrote about Roxana, he dwelt upon her eyes, which he described as "doors to another realm." Once he walked through those doors and realized he was in love with her, he woke up, just as if he'd been sleeping all his life. But it was a hopeless situation, since she was from a society that adhered to strict social codes for women. When she got pregnant, Jim and Roxana rushed off to a town near the English border that was famous for marrying secret lovers. It was so romantic, I had the chills, and that's where the pages ran out.

On the bottom of that last page was a small fruit sticker, identical to the one on the cover of *Alexander in Love*. "Made in Shangri-La." What better symbol of Grandfather's love for Roxana. But I seriously wondered if it wasn't a love that had been rotting on the branch for too long.

I replaced the pages in the envelope. "It's interesting," I said. "As far as it goes."

"There, again," Dimitris said, shaking his head in disbelief, "that's just what Oscar said."

Not far out of Afionas, an ambulance sped toward us with its lights flashing and siren wailing, forcing Mr. Moustaki onto the shoulder of the road. We exchanged looks.

"Can't you drive any faster?" I said. I couldn't believe I'd said that. "No, stop!" I shouted. "It's Dr. Vassilakis."

He was jogging along the road toward Afionas, dressed in dry-tech sports gear. He waved us on at first, but when he recognized me he flagged us down and climbed in, all out of breath, and thanked Dimitris. And off we drove again.

"Who's in the ambulance?" I asked.

"I don't know," he said. "I am out for exercise. But I'm glad to see you, Miss Hunter. I want to speak to you."

"Oh," I said. "My baby?"

"No, not at all. Your apricot." He was still huffing and puffing.

"I gave him one of Jim's," I explained to Mr. Moustaki.

From his waist pouch, Dr. Vassilakis pulled a small zip-lock baggie. It contained a fruit pit. And two tiny whitish worms.

"No way!" I gasped.

"What is it?" said Mr. Moustaki.

"They're still wriggling!" I said.

"Larvae," said Dr. Vassilakis. "Who is eating these fruits?"

"Danda, mainly," I said. "And she definitely eats the pits. She has a whole jar of them in her pantry."

"Parasites?" Moustaki asked.

"*Apomyelois ceratoniae*," said Dr. Vassilakis. "Carob moth."

We arrived as people were drifting across the road from the Kalypso Taverna to Stefanos. Georgio saw me from his patio but couldn't leave his post because men were pouring in, all worked up over something. Outside her taverna, Xenia examined a broken chair and, boy, she looked fit to kill someone. While Moustaki and Dr. Vassilakis headed for the group of men that surrounded Kostas Doukas, I joined her.

"You heard about Father Katadodis?" she asked.

"No! Was that him in the ambulance?"

"I am praying for him," she said.

"What happened?"

"It is terrible!"

"Who did it?"

"We are all to blame. Attacking him, just because he cannot do the wedding ceremony."

"You mean the priest *won't* do it. Because my grandfather won't join the church. Is that it? They attacked him for that?"

Xenia made angry fists. "Father needs to see more papers before he marries them."

"You mean documents?"

"Kostas, he is so angry he breaks a bottle on the table. But Father doesn't care. He needs to see papers from Jim's first marriage. Marriage papers he has, but where are divorce papers?"

"They didn't *get* divorced," I said. "My grandmother *died*."

"Is what I told them," she said. "Father asks, then where are her death papers?"

"Death *certificate*," I said.

"Father wants to see it. Kostas, he is so impatient he breaks my furniture. Look! It is broken. It costs thirty-seven euros, this chair. I say, 'Have your stupid meeting somewhere else!'"

Who could blame her?

"So then what happened?"

"Father was sitting—yes?—like he does, looking to the sky to ask God if he has done okay, but he is looking very pale, so he excuses himself. Danda helps Father Katadodis, and Kostas follows them, yelling. I am so embarrassed, I could kill him."

"Where is Danda?" I asked.

Xenia looked around. "She must be in the church. Is where Father had stroke."

"No way! He had a stroke?"

She put her arms around me. I don't know who was comforting whom.

"I need to find her," I said.

We found Danda near the altar, praying in the amber gloom under candlelit icons of saints. Xenia knelt beside her, snuggling close like an older sister, and whispered to her. I sat behind them, feeling strangely chilled, and then decidedly ill from the sickly sweet incense. Danda turned around to face me. Yikes! She looked like she badly needed some prayers answered.

"I too have asked your grandfather where is his wife's death certificate, to help Father," Danda whispered.

I didn't know what to say. There must have been a death certificate. And if not, a person could order another one, couldn't they?

"Jim said it is lost," Danda said. "He tells me, 'I am ordering a new one.' But where is it? It never comes. I don't think he wants to marry me."

"Of course he does," I said.

A shadow from the front door made me turn. It was Dr. Vassilakis, of course.

"He's got some news for you," I said.

She stood up, crossed herself, and with Xenia at her arm she headed to the doorway. I didn't want to watch, because I could imagine him opening his plastic bag to show them the fruit nut crawling with worms. No more apricots for Danda!

Roxana's apricots.

I felt lightheaded and hung on to the pew in front of me. Fragments of suspicion were corkscrewing around in my brain like a twister— the way Jim squirmed whenever I questioned him too much about Roxana, and his reluctance to get married—what was all that about? And now the missing death certificate, and more squirming as he lied to Danda about it. And Oscar's secret—what could be so horrible that he couldn't tell me? *My God!* I was hyperventilating, possibly going to throw up, right there in the church.

Breathe slowly, Roxy. Focus on the candle. Good. Now think of something calming. Think of Roxana Khan.

I looked up to heaven where I'd always imagined Roxana Khan watching over me, like those saints whose icons stared down at me, waiting for me to...to do what? Figure it out? One saint in particular caught my eye, a woman with sad eyes, and I thought of the girl in my grandfather's book. I was sure she was based on my grandmother, and she hadn't died in childbirth. She had given up her child to Alexander and had stayed in her valley with her apricots. Was this the secret that had driven my grandfather into a storm without a life jacket?

The idea was outrageous. Totally crazy. And then I thought of the tree. *Her* tree. Waiting for her. The one thing a girl from that valley couldn't live without. Was Grandfather hoping that she'd show up? Not now, perhaps, not after so many years. But at the time he'd planted it perhaps. Which meant what? Was this the terrible secret that Oscar was protecting? Was it even remotely possible?

Was my grandmother still alive?

I stood up and backed away from that holy spot. My head was spinning. I turned and hurried to the doorway. I needed to speak to someone immediately. But who? Oscar, sure, I wished. I couldn't wait to talk to him, if only Mr. Moustaki was ready now to return to town. Oscar would understand how I felt, and if I was wrong he would tell me point-blank and put me out of my misery. I saw Dr. Vassilakis as he wandered back to Stefanos Taverna, while Danda hurried up the pomegranate lane toward her apartment. She, of all people, I should tell. She was deep in this mess, head, heart and guts. I ran after her.

"Danda!"

She waited in her doorway and waved me inside.

"I have something to say to you too," she said. "But this is a secret what I tell you, okay?" She slammed the door and kicked off her shoes. "Sit."

I did, but she herself stayed standing, because she felt the need to plant that power fist on her hip, although I could see she was trembling.

"I'm thinking to leave this place," she said.

My heart sunk. Look what I'd caused!

"Why am I here?" she went on. "I waste my life. No marriage to Jim, no computers, no school. I am fed up!" She snapped a hand towel at a wasp that was knocking its head against the windowpane. She turned to me. "But you must tell no one."

"Your secret is safe with me," I said. "Now, you'd better sit down for mine. And hang onto something."

"I know your secret," she said. "You are in love with Georgio."

"Me? In love with Georgio?"

"You cannot fool anyone," she said, entering the kitchen.

"And how does *anyone* come to such a conclusion?" I said, following her.

"I have eyes and ears," she said.

She opened the tap to fill the kettle, but only a trickle came out. As she waited for it to fill, I could see her rib cage heaving. I backed out of the kitchen.

"Fine, I like Georgio," I consented. "You have good eyes and ears. But that's not my secret."

I heard nothing from the kitchen except the dribbling water. I sat down again, and then stood back up, I was so nervous. I could see Danda in the kitchen taking two cups and saucers from a shelf, and I waited until the clatter of setting them down had subsided.

"I think," I said, "that my grandmother might still be alive." She didn't turn around. "I don't know for sure," I said. "Perhaps I should have waited until I found out."

"Alive?" she asked. She hadn't turned around yet, but her palms were flat on the counter, like someone who had felt the house shake.

"Well, I'm not sure," I said. "What I'm saying is that she might not have died. At least, not when I thought she did. Not while giving birth to my mother. That's what I'm saying."

"Why say such stupid things?"

"To find out what you think."

"And I suppose you are happy for me to think that now I cannot marry Jim." She turned off the tap.

"This has nothing to do with that," I said. "It was you who told me about Father Katadodis wanting the death certificate. That's what convinced me. Tell me I'm wrong, if you know something, please."

She turned around. "What else do you know about this...this *woman* from Shangri-La?" Her words oozed sarcasm.

"Nothing else. Honestly. Except what I learned from reading Jim's book. Remember the pregnant girl and her apricots? She couldn't live without them."

Danda laughed mockingly at first, then nervously, as she left the kettle on the stove and stood at the window where she had a view over the Ionian Sea. She was digesting all this; you'd better believe it.

"Apricots," I said. "That was the giveaway, Grandpa and that tree of his. I know he planted his apricot tree for her."

She went to the bedroom to blow her nose, and even though I couldn't see her, I had no trouble hearing her.

"Dr. Vassilakis tells me I may be sick because of these apricots and you are telling me they are for her?"

"It's a tradition in her homeland—an apricot tree as a wedding present," I said. "I found that out yesterday."

"They belong to her?" She returned with her bottle of Pepto Bismol. "I eat them because he tends them like they are his children, and you are telling me they are for his wife? Who is alive!" She grabbed the bowl of apricots. "I don't even like these stupid little fruits! They are a curse." She marched the bowl to the doorway. "She has put a curse on me!"

Out she went with them—out the door and to the farthest corner of the stone patio. Beyond that, the land fell straight to the sea, hundreds of feet below, and that's where she hurled the apricots, bowl and all. After that, she ran back into the house and straight to the bathroom to throw up.

With the boiling water I made a cup of chamomile tea and set it by her bedside. She lay there like a corpse, which is what she must have felt like, poor woman. What an idiot I was for upsetting her like that.

"Please, don't mention this to Jim, all right?" I said. "It's my job."

She groaned.

"And if it's not true," I said, "we can both forget all about it."

Twilight had set in, and the tavernas were almost full when I gathered the courage to phone Maddy. By then Xenia's kitchen staff was creating such a clatter that I could barely hear myself speak. Not to worry, because Maddy took charge of the conversation by threatening to fly in and take me home for an abortion.

"Don't you remember why I wanted to come here in the first place?" I said. "To see my grandfather. Because he's family. I want a family, okay? Remember, we talked about it? I'm not going to get rid of this baby without thinking it through. Please, Maddy, you're making me cry."

"You should be crying, all right," she snapped. "I thought I raised you to be independent. How can you be independent when you have a baby? Smarten up!"

"I'll be the smartest mother you've ever seen," I said. "You just watch."

"Your grandfather will make you have an abortion," she said.

"Don't worry, he's trying his best, but he's got bigger problems to deal with than me."

"Like what?" she spat. "His wedding?"

"Not going to be a wedding. Are you happy?"

"Why not?"

"Because Danda will probably murder him first."

"Be serious," she said.

"I am serious. Fortunately, she's sick. She doesn't have the strength. But the village will probably take care of him."

"Well, I suppose that's a blessing," she said.

"No! I mean, the village wants to crucify him too."

"What's he done?"

I was dangerously close to talking about what I'd phoned her to talk about, but I decided that it was premature and probably irresponsible of me to bring it up. Or was I just a coward?

"It's what he *hasn't* done," I said. "Which is tell the truth."

"Oh, God, yes, the truth, by all means," she said, with the most mocking chuckle you've ever heard. "With all due respect, my darling sweetheart daughter, give me a break! What the fuck do you mean, *the truth?*"

"Maybe if you'd gotten his letters, you'd know," I said.

"I told you, honey, there were no letters. You think I haven't ransacked her house for your goddamned letters!"

"Honestly, Maddy, do you think she was going to save them? Was she that stupid?"

Big pause while we both tried to plumb the depths of Gretchen's depravity.

"Letters saying what?" Maddy snapped.

"How should I know? They were probably about Grandmother!"

That's as far as I was going, full stop, not another word.

"What are you talking about? What about Grandmother?"

"I'll know tomorrow," I said. "I'm going to make Grandfather tell me, or else. Then I'll tell you."

"Tell me now!"

"No," I said, "I don't know."

"But it was in those letters, you said."

"I don't know," I said. "I shouldn't have told you anything."

"Something Aunt Gretchen would have known?" she asked.

"I don't know! Just forget it."

"I'll rip her house apart, girl, I swear to God. You know what else I found? Deposits into her bank account, every year on my birthday. My birthday! I'll kill her!"

"She's already dead, Maddy."

She didn't even say goodbye.

Across the street, on the lamp-lit patio at Stefanos, Georgio was busy charming a group of Americans.

"Hey, Roxy!"

He ran across the road. "You come see my friends, okay? Big movie coming to Afionas."

His so-called friends were location scouts for a production of some sort. Georgio was so excited. I stood up and gave him a little kiss on the cheek.

"I'm going to sleep," I said.

He cupped his hand around my face. "Later I come kiss you goodnight," he said.

"That would be nice," I said, trying to sound casual, but the quiver in my voice gave me away.

He smiled in a way I'd never seen before, and when he kissed me I didn't care that those Americans were watching.

It was after midnight and I still couldn't sleep, couldn't get Maddy out of my mind. She *would* tear Gretchen's house apart, quite literally, but would she find anything? Hijacking somebody's mail is one thing, but saving it! How awful. A person's entire life based on a lie—it was possible. It was actually possible. I felt dangerously claustrophobic, like I might need to run out into the night.

I heard a knock on my door. It was him, Georgio. Thank God! I grabbed him, and like two fugitives we slipped downstairs and out a side door. He took me by the hand, but it was me pulling him up the road and across a moonlit meadow to the top of the terraced hillside. Within the orchard, a dim glow reflecting off the chalky trail was all we had to go by as I followed Georgio, skipping downward, terrace to terrace. What a relief to get out of my head. I felt so free, running with the one person who accepted me for who I was.

We came to a stone hut, very primitive, built into the slope and dark as a tomb. He slipped inside and returned with a plastic bottle.

"Retsina," he said.

"What?" I asked.

"Wine," he said. "Is good."

I tried it: cold, almost icy. But I spit it out.

"Yuck! Are you trying to poison me? What's in there?"

"Retsina."

"Not for me your retsina wine," I said.

We plopped down on a wooden bench against the hut's stone wall, barely visible to each other, like ghosts, our legs touching.

"Hey, guess what is this," and he started humming and bum-ba-dumming a tune.

"*Star Wars*?" I asked.

"Bravo!" he shouted.

"My turn," I said, and gave him what I thought was a brilliant version of *Lord of the Rings*.

He listed off a dozen different movies, making a mess of the titles, and pretty soon we were laughing our heads off. I couldn't believe how comfortable we were with each other, which is relationship gold, right?

Okay, this could work, this kind of easygoing connection with a guy, I thought. *You can't invent that kind of thing, you can't buy it for a million dollars.*

Then Georgio started up about his mother.

"Are you sure you want to go there?"

"Yes, I went there," he said.

It turned out that *there* was a mental hospital in Athens where his mother was virtually imprisoned for having attacked Stefanos with a knife.

I knew it!

"Your mother," I said, "what is she like?"

I was watching to see if the question made him uncomfortable.

"She no like to wear shoes," he said.

"That's called being a free spirit," I said.

"She is in Greek army," he said.

"She was?" Free spirit and army boots seemed to me like a bad match.

"She like to tell stories," Georgio said, "and sing songs."

"Do you remember one?"

He started singing, his eyes closed. A kindred orphan trying to conjure up his mother's love. I didn't understand a word. I was speechless.

After a long silence, I took hold of his hand and said, "The ones left behind suffer the most."

"You want I sing you again?"

"Not if it's going to make you sad," I said.

He began another precious lament, and pretty soon I could hear tears on his lips. I didn't want him emotionally naked because I know how boys handle embarrassment—not well at all—and I feared that we'd wind up never seeing each other again. I squeezed his hand, hoping it would shut him up.

"You will marry me?"

"Shut up!" I laughed, which I shouldn't have, but what was I going to say?

"In five years taverna is mine. We change name to *Roxana's*, okay?"

"Or *Shangri-La*," I said.

"Okay!" he said.

I couldn't believe I was leading him on like that, but I was becoming turned on to this future he was proposing. This island was the perfect place to raise my baby, safe from all the threats of disaster in the world that Maddy was always warning me about.

"I've been thinking a lot about you," I said.

"What you are thinking?"

And that's when I kissed him. I kissed him so passionately that I lost my breath. I'd expected him to tear the meat off my bones, as boys do, but no, it was weird, he wanted to look at me, and he traced his fingertips lightly along my eyebrow and down my face. His dark eyes were like polished stones in the moonlight, no shifting here and there, not a quiver, not a doubt. If it was a trap, I was dead meat, because I kissed him again. He remained the perfect gentleman, responding to every move I made but never pushing further, until finally I ran out of kisses.

"Georgio, do you like me?"

His eyes searched mine, and without speaking he led me away from the hut. Just a few steps over to soft ground under a tree, we lowered ourselves onto a bed of olive leaves.

"No rush, okay?" I whispered.

He kissed me, gently, and then began a kissing journey down my chest to my tummy, unbuttoning my shirt as he went. Why had I said, no rush? I grabbed him and pulled him on top of me, and I might as well have poured a bucket of cold water over him, because he just quit. He slid off to lie beside me, letting his hand lazily stroke down from my throat to my belly button. It was driving me crazy.

"Am I coming on too strong?" I asked, rolling over to face him.

"You are very strong," he said.

"Sorry."

He smiled, and I giggled, and then he chuckled. We were still good, thank God, and I melted into him again.

"I love you, Georgio," I said.

How was I to know that that was the trigger? Too late for second thoughts; I was on my back. I felt his desperation as if it was my own, as if both of us were bursting with things that needed to be said. I wanted him to know my secret. I could feel it burning inside me, could feel my baby. Could he feel it too? I had to tell him now before it was too late. But how?

I started to cry. "I'm sorry."

"I no understand," he said.

"Me neither."

Every dumb word, every kiss and touch arose from nowhere. Everything was unfolding perfectly for us shipwrecked lovers, two accidental secret keepers floating away in each other's arms.

It was almost dawn when I said, "Georgio? What do you know about my grandmother?"

His cheek rested on my belly, as if he and my baby were having a secret conversation. I could feel his heart and the cool of his face, so that if he had tried to con me with some BS, I would have known it immediately.

"You can tell me the truth now," I said. "What happened to my grandmother?" I felt his face get hot.

"She go home," he said.

"What do you mean?"

"She leave Jim. Go back home."

It was a punch in the gut all over again. I was right. *Roxana had not died. My grandmother had not died in childbirth.*

"She went home?" I said. "To her own people?"

His tears laced their way around my waist. Why was he crying? Because he'd betrayed his Uncle Jim? I stroked his head, hoping he'd realize that Jim would forgive him for opening his vault of secrets. Or were they tears of joy? He should have been happy for Jim that his secret was finally out in the open.

"There will be no more secrets, I promise you, no more secrets."

Reluctantly he told me more, about Roxana's father showing up and taking Roxana back with him.

"So did Jim follow her?" I asked. "Or did Roxana bring the baby back?"

"No, she not come back."

"Then how did Uncle Jim get little Matabhan? She was my mother, you know."

"Roxana, she no take the baby with her."

"Shut up!" I said. "The baby was tiny. She wouldn't just leave her. She wouldn't do that, Georgio. You've got it wrong, I'm sorry."

He continued to spill tears all over my tummy, which meant he actually believed this pile-of-crap story, but there was no doubt about his compassion for Uncle Jim. It infected me too, the idea that Jim was a victim in all this. I didn't have the heart to ask Georgio how it all happened. I just stroked his head.

"You will marry me, yes?"

"Ssshh," I said.

I wasn't sure about my heart at all. I wasn't sure about anything anymore.

The first grey shards of dawn were cutting jagged holes in the canopy of olive leaves above me.

16

Blood, Sweat and Axes

Noon, and I was moody as thunder. Last night's tears had not evaporated with the rising sun; quite the contrary. But neither had the thrill of our lovemaking and the memory of how close we'd been for hours. Yes, Georgio had made me happier than I'd ever been, but I could not believe that Grandma had abandoned her baby.

My morning "kali mera" to Xenia was not accompanied by its usual smile, yet she still had to make a language lesson out of it, telling me it was "*eeneh oraya mera*," a beautiful day. And it was too, blissfully blue, and just waiting for someone like me to ruin it for her. I could barely prevent myself from saying, "Oh, and by the way, Xenia, it turns out my grandmother is alive. Sorry about that."

I had to talk to Grandfather before this thing leaked out. God knows what Danda would do to him if she got there first— probably hurl him over the cliff along with those apricots. And Georgio needed to know the truth about me before our relationship progressed another millimeter. The problem was his brothers—they were hanging out at Stefanos' entrance like guards.

It was a challenge to slip away from Xenia's without Georgio's radar picking me up, but I managed it, all the way to Danda's door. I needed reassurance that she was still too sick to visit Jim, because I wanted to be the first to confront him. Sure enough, she was in bed, and looking worse than ever. Her problem wasn't the parasites but Dr. Vassilakis' prescription. The pills were killing everything inside her, including her will to live. When I told her I intended to talk to Jim, she said, "Bring me my axe."

"We're going to kill him?" I asked.

"I am so happy you said *we*," she said, trying to sit up. "We are sisters now."

She was serious. She wanted me to fetch the axe from the patio. So I did. She wanted me to hold it "as if your life depended on it."

"I couldn't actually kill anyone," I said.

"But you can feel something, holding it, yes?"

Oh yeah, I felt like a murderer. I could have busted something to smithereens, starting with the curse on our family, those lies that had ruined our lives.

"Yes, Roxy, that feeling," she said. "Put it in your heart."

If she only knew how long it had been there already.

"We must learn to defend what is in our hearts," Danda continued. "I teach my girls to speak well, with language that can become as powerful as an axe."

She reached out and tested the blade with her finger. It was frightening.

"Thank you for coming to see me," she said, looking revived. In fact, she rose from bed to see me to the door.

I left, convinced that she was right about having an axe standing by in your heart. It stood for the truth. If a man couldn't take the truth, then too bad.

I had Stefanos Taverna in my sights when Xenia emerged from the Kalypso across the street and hurried to intercept me.

"I have bad news for Jim," she said.

"Today's the day for bad news," I said.

"Oscar Hartmann is dead," she said.

"No! When?"

"Yesterday."

"No!"

"I'm sorry."

"How?" I asked.

"I don't know."

I felt my face begin to crumple, and ran toward the taverna. But I knew I couldn't face anyone, so I kept running farther up the road out of town, already crying. When I heard a vehicle approaching, I took a trail that lead into the orchard and collapsed under a tree.

Oscar. *No!* He was the only one who understood anything. I would never forget him. And I admired him for the way he swore an oath and remained true to it to the end. They didn't make people like that anymore.

I smelled smoke and sat up. I heard the dull thudding of an axe, which directed my gaze a short distance into the orchard where an elderly couple tended a fire. The old woman was chopping debris; the blunt chunk-chunk of her axe in the hard old wood set my mind to fantasizing about chopping down a tree.

Is that why Danda wanted the axe? To cut down the apricot tree. It couldn't be, could it? The axe was only a symbol, a metaphor to make her point, her philosophy lesson. Or was it? Or was it!

I started back, still groggy, still unsure, then ran for it. I kept seeing the look in Danda's eye as she rose from her sickbed, and the more I recalled it, the more horrified I became, since I realized what she planned to do with the axe.

Xenia must have heard me galloping down the road, because she emerged from the taverna, calling my name. The last thing I needed was Georgio running out to talk to me, so I ran faster, past Stefanos. Once past the church and out of sight around a couple of bends in the lane, I slowed down to catch my breath, and that's when I heard footsteps behind me. I took off again, but didn't get far, not even to the herb fields before he caught me.

"Georgio, I have to get to Jim's!" I pleaded. "Something awful is going to happen."

"I come with you."

"Not right now. I'll see you later, okay?"

"Please, you must tell to me."

"Tell you what?"

"What I ask you last night."

"Sorry, Georgio, not now. Later, okay?"

"You no like last night."

"I *loved* last night. Oh, Georgio—I know, we have to talk, and we will."

"My brothers, they say you no love me."

"Tell your brothers they are wrong."

"Theo say you will not marry me."

"Georgio, there's something I have to tell you."

It was clear that the only route to Jim's house lay on the other side of telling Georgio the truth. The open doorway of Xenia's wine shed seemed made for the occasion, so I pulled Georgio into the dark and yeasty shadows.

"Are you listening?" I asked.

"I am listen."

"Okay, here's something for you to think about." I placed my hands on my tummy. "I'm pregnant."

"Baby?" he said. I couldn't believe it, his eyes actually brightened. Boys weren't supposed to appreciate this kind of thing. You can't imagine what a huge relief it was.

"Baby, yes, but listen to me, Georgio—"

"Then we marry, yes?"

"Marry?" I repeated. I couldn't believe it. I knew he was perfect, but I hadn't imagined he was a saint.

"Of course!" he said.

Oh, my God. He thought the baby was his.

"No, no, no. The baby isn't yours, Georgio."

His luminous face went drab as a warehouse wall.

"No, Georgio, please, listen to me. It's somebody else's, a boy I'm not in love with, I promise you. I'm not marrying him. I'll never even see him again, ever."

I'd never seen the shell-shocked Georgio.

"Say something," I said.

Silence.

"I'm sorry, Georgio. I'm so sorry. That's what we have to talk about." He was hurt worse than I thought. "Come here, Georgio."

I pulled him farther into the shed, dying to have his arms around me, but he shoved me away, then rushed out and slammed the door, leaving me in total darkness. It wouldn't open, and if there was a handle, I couldn't find it.

"Georgio! Open the door!" I listened. Nothing. "I'm frightened!" I was dripping with sweat. "It's dark in here!"

The darkness resounded with a sharp crash. He must have kicked the door.

"Is that you, Georgio? I tried to tell you before, honestly, I did! I love you!"

I was praying that it was actually him outside the door. It opened abruptly, the sunlight blinding me. I stepped out where I could see him and, boy, did he look ill. I reached for his hand, which he snatched back. Then he kicked the door and marched down the lane toward the village. My heart sank, then rose up in anger.

"Georgio!"

He wasn't coming back, not a chance.

I picked up a stone, but couldn't bring myself to throw it at him. Why was I so scared of hurting everyone when I was getting hurt all the time? All the time!

I ran toward the herb fields, so totally lost in my own misery that I only came to my senses as I was sliding down the escarpment without the help of Georgio's rope. I might have killed myself. And maybe I wouldn't have even cared, not just because Georgio had rejected me, but because I felt numb. Dead to the world.

And my hand was bleeding. *Perfect!*

Standing there on that little neck of sand, I had never felt farther from anyone who cared about me. I seriously thought about rowing off in Georgio's boat. But what was the point? I already felt all washed up. Right there on the very same spot where Odysseus had found himself. Where some fancy princess came along and rescued him. I couldn't see one in sight. I actually looked around, how pathetic is that? And that's when the sadness came raining down on me. *I'll never make a good mother*, I thought. I wasn't grown up enough, wasn't that painfully obvious? How could I think of perpetuating this sadness in the life of another child?

I heard voices coming from the house. It sounded like arguing. By any measure of decency, I should have left them to fight it out in private, but what did I care? Anyway, their arguments hardly interested me. I was listening for the sound of an axe.

They were in the apricot courtyard—what better place for a showdown with James Bearsden. As I approached, I realized that he was doing most of the yelling, but beating himself up. The old remorse tactic works magic on a woman, apparently. Danda's tone resembled more of a purr than a growl, and soon they mewed like a couple of kittens. *Nice work, Danda!* Then I heard the axe fall to the ground and, after that, silence.

I tiptoed to the archway, half expecting to see a decapitated tree, but there it was all open arms as usual. Except nothing was as usual anymore, nor would be ever again. Not Georgio, certainly not poor Oscar. Not me either. Not even that tree. That big lie spoiled everything, especially Roxana's tree, which wasn't looking so beneficent anymore, not so blessed, not at all. In fact, it could almost be blamed, the way it had stood there for years, driving Grandfather crazy. I couldn't blame Danda for chickening out, given what she stood to lose—the school, her computers, her modern girls of Greece. Maddy and me, we'd already lost everything, so it made perfect sense to find me at his door demanding answers. Seventeen years with an axe in my heart; I deserved some answers!

I wanted to start yelling, but couldn't. I'd gone through life without daring to disturb anyone, handing out Kleenex to everyone but myself. Ever since I could remember, I'd been trying to emulate my saintly grandmother who gave her life for her child. But now it turns out she had a life after all. So where was *my* life? Nothing seemed to have a heartbeat anymore except that monstrous lie.

I picked up the axe. It shocked me, how menacing it felt in my hand, and how crystal clear my mind was, and how clearly I could see and hear. There were murmurs from the back room, as if suddenly life was back to normal, which it totally wasn't. As if I wasn't standing out there with an axe. As if my mother hadn't become an orphan for no reason. As if Oscar Hartmann wasn't dead. As if hundreds or thousands of people weren't standing in line waiting to be told the truth—agents, publishers, lawyers, friends and readers, and me at the head of that line feeling almighty with an axe in my hand. *The truth!* I swung the axe. I swung it again and again and again. It was lunacy to blame that tree, but all I felt was rage.

The boughs were secured to the white wall so that the tree couldn't fall over, and when I finally chopped through its trunk, it sprung upward and nearly took my head off. That's when I totally lost it, and bashed it off the wall until it lay on the ground like a monster in rigor mortis.

"Oh, my God!" I gasped.

Bark fragments stuck to the wall, leaving a ghostly outline as if Roxana were there watching—watching over me with total compassion. I'd never felt more powerful or alive in all my life.

"What are you doing!" Danda stood in the doorway, shocked, the buttons of her dress done up all wrong. She reached for the axe, but I jerked it away so abruptly that it grazed my ear. She grabbed for it again, and as I jumped back I noticed a thread of blood dance in the air before it became a gory red tentacle on the pristine wall. We wrestled with the axe until a branch tripped us up and we fell to the ground together, neither of us letting go.

"No more need for the axe," Danda said, barely able to breathe. "Jim is bleeding already. Please, you come and see."

She got to her feet and offered me her hand, which I refused. But I rushed to bar the doorway so she couldn't re-enter the house. I still held the axe.

"You had your time with him," I said. "Now's my turn."

"We should let him rest, okay? Please, Roxy? I can tell you what he said."

"No! I have my own questions to ask him."

Danda stared at me without any malice whatsoever. "You're bleeding, did you know?" she said.

Blood was dripping onto my shoulder.

Then Danda moved away from the doorway and gave me a look that seemed to say, *Go girl!* She gathered up her shoes, and walked off toward the beach.

The air was heavy with apricot essence leaking from all those broken limbs. It was like a crime scene, seriously, complete with blood splattered on the wall, dripping down my arm and sticky in my hand as I held tight to the axe.

I stepped into the house and stood in the middle of the living room, listening. Through the window, I could see Danda hurrying across the isthmus. On Jim's desk, a piece of paper protruded from the typewriter—and beside the typewriter a small candle was burning in front of a framed photo of Oscar. Grandfather knew. What's more, the ribbon was installed in the typewriter, threaded up and ready to go. He'd been writing again.

I heard his voice from the bedroom.

"Yes? Hello? Hello?" he was saying. "Can ye please speak up?"

I tried his door latch and pushed it open. He was using a cellphone—my phone.

"Yes, I'm looking for...hello? I'm looking for someone—I'm not entirely sure she's still with us—a woman by the name of Roxana Khan."

Grandfather noticed me. I was still holding the axe, from which blood was dripping onto the floor. It must have looked more than a little melodramatic, but I didn't care. He kept talking.

"No, son, I assumed ye're not the headman. Your father is...ahh, I see. He's not in? And Roxana Khan is not in either?"

Whoa! She's alive!

"Very well, I'll call back." Jim was about to hang up when he said, "Do we have what? Email? No, no email at this address, I'm afraid."

"Yes!" I interrupted. "I have email."

He handed me the phone.

167

"Hi," I said into the phone. "That was my grandfather. Your name is what? Mohammed? Cool. My name's Roxy."

Grandfather waved his arms as a warning against saying too much, but Mohammed was only asking me if Roxy was short for Roxana. Anyway, I gave him my email address.

"I will send a message the moment Grandmama returns," Mohammed said.

"Your grandmother?"

"The lady you are calling for," he said in his perfect English. "Roxana Khan."

Roxana Khan is his grandmother!

"She is making the rounds of the villages delivering babies. She returns in a fortnight."

Fortnight? I thanked him and hung up.

Grandfather was no longer in the room. From the bedroom doorway I saw him in the courtyard taking stock of the catastrophe. I was prepared to be blasted right off the map of Greece, but then I heard him say, "Solar panels," quite matter-of-factly. I moved closer. "They're going on the roof," he continued. I must have shrugged, because he gave it to me again with both barrels. "Those goddamned solar panels, damn it! They're going on the damn roof!"

He marched into the house and straight to his desk where he opened a drawer and withdrew his chequebook and spread it open. He shouted for Danda as he scrawled violently on one of the cheques.

"She's not here," I said.

"She talks about computers all day long—fine! Let's get one of those damn things!" He ripped the cheque out and smacked it down on the desk. "And you, young lady, you're goin' to teach me how to use it. For heaven's sake, clean yerself up. Have ye seen yerself?"

No way he was shifting the attention onto me. He knew darn well what I wanted to hear: *Grandmother had not died.* He'd stewed in his big lie for most of his life, and still he was stewing and hemming and hawing and fidgeting until finally he pulled a fat brown envelope full of pages out of the drawer and plopped it onto his desk with a little flick of the hand, as if to say, *Take the damn thing.* I hated to spoil the sheets of paper with my bloody fingers, but I did. I flipped through them and saw immediately how he'd continued the Roxana tragedy, how she'd been forcibly taken back to Kashmir. From the crispness of the pages, I could tell they were fresh from his typewriter. And watching all this from within his little seashell picture frame was Oscar, seeming so pleased.

"I'm going to read this," I said. I inserted the pages into the envelope and laid it respectfully on his typewriter. "But we still have to talk."

He glared at me, then at the envelope smeared with my blood. "It's all there, what yer wantin' to know."

"But you have to actually tell me," I said. "You need to tell me the story."

His eyes shifted left and right, his whole being as prickly with panic as a cornered raccoon, and he stood up. I thought he was going to push past me, but instead he snatched the axe from my hand and brought it down on the typewriter. That old contraption bounced a foot into the air, its thousand little levers and springs exploding in all directions as it cartwheeled off the desk. The spool of typewriter ribbon flew across the room like an exorcised demon. He would've slammed that machine again, except he couldn't shake the axe blade free of the envelope—it was skewered like a kabob—and then he let go of the axe and rubbed his back as if he'd strained it. He looked at his hands. They shook terribly and were sticky red. His nose was running too. He touched the scar on the back of his head, as if something might be leaking there, like the truth.

"We were married, ye know that," he grumbled.

I knew that already, so I waited. His breathing became laboured.

"I know you were married," I finally said, trying my hardest not to upset him. "And nobody knew about it. Did her parents know about the baby?"

"No, of course not! Can you imagine what they'd do?"

"But you had to tell them eventually. And you were married, so it's not like you did anything wrong."

"Ye have to understand, Roxy. She'd turned her back on them.

Her family, her entire culture."

"So you were keeping the whole thing a secret," I said. It figured. "Then what happened? Please, Grandfather, I know already."

"Well, then, ye know," he said.

"No, tell me."

"She left me."

There it was. She left. She didn't die, she left. I knew it, but there it was, finally, from his own mouth. The veil of lies that separated Maddy and me from who we really were had finally been lifted. So why didn't I feel relieved? I was still angry.

"She had the baby and then she left?" I said.

"Aye, after a spell."

"Excuse me, but I find that hard to believe."

"I'm tellin' ye."

"Well, where did she go?" I asked.

"Home."

"You mean, back to her valley?"

"Aye."

Hardly an enthusiastic confession. More like pulling teeth without any freezing.

"Why?"

"Her mother was very sick. She wanted to see Roxanna for one last time. Her father came to Scotland to fetch her back."

"She left without the baby? My grandmother wouldn't do that."

"You're absolutely right," he said. "She didna want to, but she did, poor gerl. Try to imagine her state. Her mother is on her deathbed: was that the time to tell them about being married and having a child?"

"So you're saying she left the baby behind?"

I could see his face tighten, emotion working overtime to transform him into a human being. "Aye."

"With you?" I asked.

"Who else? I had Gretchen to help me."

"And she didn't come back?"

He got shifty-eyed again. I thought he might try to make a run for it, so I stepped toward him.

"Ye don't understand! She couldna come back, Roxy!" He looked desperate.

I crouched in front of him and took one of his hands, which shook fiercely. I gave it a little squeeze.

"They wouldna let her, would they? If someone had stabbed me in the back," he said, "I would have thought it was my heart breaking."

Whoa.

The cat jumped into his lap, and that did it. He held it like a baby, choking back tears. I knelt in front of him.

"She had no idea that she wouldn't be coming back," I said. "Is that it?"

The look on his face startled me. Something inside him had changed. I didn't want to stare, so I laid my head on his knee, eye to eye with that apricot cat, and I thought, *Okay, this is good, this is really, really good. Grandpa is with us now. The gods have brought him home.*

When I lifted my head, he was looking at me—I mean, *really* looking at me.

"Tell me everything," I said.

17

Party Interruptus

Straining and growling, higher and higher, that never-say-die old bus that's destined for Shangri-La miraculously keeps going and going.

"This bus reminds me of Grandfather," I say.

"You mean it's going to break down?" she says.

Maddy is a nervous wreck, what with no sleep and the worry of meeting her mother, and the bus ride. Rough! Not to mention the altitude, since we're up over three thousand metres. The air's getting thin up here.

"Grandfather was like a camel," I say, "carrying that huge load."

"Every camel has a limit," Maddy says. I can tell that she's worrying about the bus crapping out. "At some point, one more straw breaks its back."

Who knows which small straw broke my grandfather? What forced him to finally plug himself back into the real world? Mohammed humiliating him for not having email? Perhaps it was the prospect of speaking to Roxana after all this time. It might have been the promise of weight lifted *off* his shoulders, the big lie he no longer had to carry around. For that we can thank Oscar. For dying. Horrible thing to say, I know. But once Oscar was gone, Jim couldn't dishonour his memory by continuing with his old intransient ways. He had to start writing. It was a win-win situation, though, with Oscar winning the gravestone and Jim winning his life back.

As for me, I hadn't known if I would be able to survive a fortnight, which I'd learned meant two weeks. Mohammed and I arranged everything by email, not that I breathed a word to him about who Jim Bearsden really was. Or who I was, for that matter. The plan was simply that Roxana would phone "an old friend" on his wedding day, that's how I explained it to Mohammed. Roxana, of course, would understand immediately.

Once he got wired, Grandfather couldn't get modern fast enough, couldn't finish that memoir quickly enough. We took turns at the keyboard, typing his monologue into the latest laptop technology, which featured a sound effect that made it click-clack like Ernest Hemingway's old Underwood typewriter. What a laugh we got out of that. We kept three batteries charging up at Danda's apartment until Georgio got "those damn solar panels" installed on Uncle Jim's roof. The basket brigade ran the batteries back and forth, along with his daily croissants, tomatoes, cheese, olives and whatnot. Jim needed me around to teach him the word processing program, but mainly, he said, to remind him who he was writing it for.

I have a copy of the manuscript with me on the bus. Roxana agreed to add a postscript, and then the memoir will be published. Trust Maddy to get wound up for not being asked to write a chapter too. I convinced her that her own life was worth a screenplay of its own, since here she was, a thirty-six-year-old woman about to meet her mother for the first time.

"You're finally in a movie with a happy ending," was how I broke the news to her.

At every twist in the road, Maddy clutches my hand. I kiss her on the cheek, which calms her down for about four seconds. Up ahead, the valley widens at last. It's been a vertical landscape for hours. Level ground is so scarce up here that crops are cultivated on little terraced plots, every smudge of green a miracle, and every boulder on the road a reminder of how our lives could be snuffed out at any minute.

Maddy must have noticed the same thing, because she clutches my hand again.

"Only an hour to go," I tell her. From the looks of her, that's fifty-nine minutes too long. "Unless we're killed by an avalanche," I say.

"Don't say that."

"Well, Grandfather almost was. When he came after her, right? One mile further up the road and he'd have been wiped out."

She's not listening, too busy trying not to hurl, poor thing.

"Look, Mom! The apricot trees."

There they are below us, on little terraces, the apricot orchards of Shangri-La. You can see how they're irrigated by stone aqueducts built along the side of the valley, the icy water channeled down from the glaciers. Maddy glances out the window and sighs, woefully uninterested, then shuts her eyes again. Even now she doesn't understand Jim's apricot obsession, and of course she arrived too late to see the infamous wedding tree. Too late for the wedding, as well. And she nearly missed the party, thanks to arriving at the last possible minute. Typical Maddy.

According to Georgio, Afionas had never staged such a bash, with both tavernas joining forces to prepare a feast that lasted two days— starting the day before with a solar panel party at Jim's house. The official switching-on took place in his welcoming courtyard, a little light illuminating a mural on the white wall: the image of an apricot tree painted by Rebecca Moustaki.

Up in the village, the party lasted through the night and into the wedding day. I managed a nap between six and ten a.m., but woke with Danda on my mind, worried that she might be fretting over Maddy and Jim's reunion. Would it upstage her wedding? I found her conspiring with Xenia over bouquet arrangements.

"All Jim's ghosts should be at the wedding," Danda said. "We will make them drunk on Xenia's wine. Roxana should be here too."

"Ssshh," I said. "The village doesn't know about her."

That was the final glitch: Roxana's death certificate. It arrived at the last minute, from the hand of Mr. Moustaki directly into the hands of Father Katadodis, who barely glanced at it. He'd lost the sight in one eye, due to his stroke, and at this point couldn't have cared less that the document was fake. If Danda wasn't worried, then no one else in the village was worried. Nobody much cared about anything except Jim being delivered to the altar before the summer was over.

The town had quadrupled in size overnight. Dr. Vassilakis and Moustaki's legal buddies came in from Corfu town, along with farmers and waiters and writers from all over the island. There were even three monks from the nearby monastery. But the biggest surprise was Jim and Oscar's fan club. At first, I thought it was a vanload of wannabe writers, but these were the now grown-up children that Jim and Oscar had been reading to at the Corfu library for over twenty-five years. I corralled them into Stefanos Taverna to help with the sanitizing project. Vats of boiling water were deployed to dissolve layer upon layer of gunk on the wooden cutting boards and counter tops.

Georgio and I had called a ceasefire on account of the massive wedding prep still to do. It took us a day just to string coloured lights across the street between the two tavernas. Georgio wouldn't let me climb the step ladder, and once when he was up there he got tears in his eyes, though it couldn't have been because he loved me, because he hated me, and who could blame him, since it must have appeared to him as if I was trying to dupe him, saddling him with a baby that wasn't his.

"When is baby?" he asked.

I was so afraid of that question. I was afraid because the answer demanded a commitment from me, one way or the other, and I was still prevaricating. Catching myself with a maternal hand on my tummy, I quickly removed it, then felt like the worst traitor.

"We've got work to do, Georgio," I said.

"When baby comes," he said, "I will take him to go fish."

I turned away so that he wouldn't see my tears. Boy, they were set to deluge, so I ran to my room at the Kalypso where I unscrewed a light bulb from the ceiling, then returned with it to Georgio's kitchen where I begged him to replace the greasy one.

Let there be light!

"If we're changing the name to Roxana's," I said, testing his sense of humour, "the cook has to see what he's doing."

He gave me a cynically raised eyebrow, which I took as a very positive sign. The real Georgio was more adorable than ever.

"We have to be able to breathe in here too, okay?"

He went to work opening the one small kitchen window, and accidentally smashed it. I wanted to kiss him so badly, to make him smile, but I settled for helping him scour the stove. It felt like therapy, the two of us pouring our energy into renewing a greasy old stove.

"Look," he said. "Is made by Pitsos."

I scrubbed a little harder. "In Athens," I said.

He wiped a smudge of grime off my cheek.

Meanwhile, the volunteers scrubbed the floor until an Art Deco pattern emerged on the tiles. We sterilized every dish and utensil and didn't return them to their drawers until the drawers themselves were scrubbed outside under the midday sun where Georgio could see for himself what vermin thrived amongst his knives and forks. We bleached those little bastards to kingdom come.

On the afternoon of the second day, they got married in the church. Danda wore a hot dress hidden beneath a politically correct shawl. Rows of plaster saints stared down on all of us, more than making up for anything Father Katadodis may have missed by having only one good eye. Jim looked ten years younger in a linen suit, pink shirt, trimmed beard and Panama hat. I gave him away.

The ceremony was conducted in Greek, so don't ask me what was said, but they did everything three times—rings held over their heads, drinking from a cup, and circling around a table with crowns on their heads. Jim and Danda kissed like two penguins rubbing beaks. It was awesome.

It was more awesome seeing Georgio cry.

I felt badly that Maddy hadn't arrived in time to see it.

It was twilight, with the party in high gear and Stefanos strumming his manic little bouzouki, Georgio dancing for the bride and groom and everyone else singing and clapping. Mr. Moustaki tapped me on the shoulder. He was holding his cellphone. I immediately thought, *Uh-oh, Maddy's not coming*, but he led me away from the mayhem and a short ways up the dark road where he stopped and pointed to a parked taxi. He handed me the phone.

"You're kidding," I said. I put my ear to the receiver. "Maddy? Is that you?"

"Hi, sweetie."

I handed him back the phone and ran toward the car where I could see her getting out. I ran into her arms the way I did when I was five years old. I couldn't get enough of staring at her, she seemed like an alien. The tendons in her neck were ropes.

"What?"

"Nothing," I said.

"Not nothing," she said.

She was right, just looking at her made me realize how long I'd been away, and how much had happened.

"You look terrible," I said.

"So would you," she whispered, "after a night in Mr. Moustaki's hotel."

"I know!" I said, and we laughed. It was great! "You can freshen up in my room, come on." Taking her by the hand was like pulling a mule. "That's him singing," I said. "He's getting drunk."

"Oh, sweetie, I'm not sure I can do this."

I wasn't sure that I could either. It felt weird, leading Maddy by the hand to do what she and her father should have done ages ago. Their love should have been the foundation of this family, something a child takes for granted. When I let go of her, she continued to inch her way forward until we stood at the perimeter of the party.

"That's not him, is it?" she asked.

"Yes! Isn't he great? And that's Georgio dancing with him. Georgio, my friend."

The look she gave me, disapproval overwhelmed by total helplessness—I loved it. I mean, there was her father, whom she had virtually no memory of, and who was supposed to be in a coma but was instead dancing with Danda Skandalidis resplendent in a white dress cut astonishingly low. As for Maddy, I'd never seen her look so vulnerable, like she'd landed on another planet.

"You know, sweetie, I should wait until tomorrow," she said. "I would just ruin it, don't you think?"

"Maybe," I said.

Jim raised his glass and shouted, "To Danda! Yassou!" followed by a bunch of blah-blah about how he wouldn't have recovered without her, and how without her the Afionas Primary School would be in the Dark Ages—whatever made people applaud and drink, that's what the celebration was about. Danda thanked somebody or other, and Xenia toasted the mayor for who-knows-what; it was all Greek to me. Georgio kissed his father and said something that brought tears to the old man's eyes. Then, to my huge surprise, Father Katadodis mentioned my name. He thanked God in English for my arrival in Afionas. Of course, people looked around to locate me as the priest pressed on, something to the effect that I'd brought the love of family back into Uncle Jim's heart. Kostas banged his beer bottle on the table and spoke of Father Katadodis, acknowledging his faith, which, let's face it, had been rock-solid through some pretty rude meetings. Jim then asked the priest to bless his chequebook, which he spread open on the table in front of him like a peace treaty.

"What's he doing?" Maddy said, gripping my hand.

"Spending your inheritance. But it's okay. It's going to a good cause. Children. Girls, mainly."

She relaxed a bit.

Danda leaned over Jim's shoulder to help him correctly fill in the amount, while Dimitris whispered in his other ear—some financial advice, probably. Father Katadodis was performing his ritualistic blessing over this historic signing when Xenia tapped me on the shoulder.

"Someone for you, Roxy, on the phone."

"Who?"

"A lady doctor with a very nice accent," she said.

Doctor? Accent? *Oh, my God! It's Grandmother!* But what was she doing asking for *me*? "She asked for me?"

"Who is it?" Xenia asked.

In all the anticipation of expecting Roxana's call, I'd forgotten the danger it posed. No one was supposed to know about her, because everyone thought she was dead! I grabbed Maddy's hand and pulled her with me toward the taverna.

"What?"

"Just come!" I pulled her with me.

Music from Xenia's sound system made it nearly impossible to hear or be heard over the phone, but I couldn't just stand there holding the receiver.

"Hello," I said.

"Hello," came the voice. "Who is speaking, please?"

It was her voice. *Her voice.* I couldn't believe it; it was like a voice from the grave. It was a miracle.

"This is Roxy," I said.

"Mohammed tells me you're Jim's granddaughter."

"Please, wait one minute," I said. I was going to faint or cry, I didn't know which, so I handed Maddy the phone.

"Who is it?" Maddy said.

"It's *her*. Say something."

Maddy, phone to her ear, wiped away the tears that were streaming down her face.

"Say hello, or she'll hang up," I said.

You've never seen such a face, joy melting the lines on the map of her tired features, the extreme makeover to end all makeovers. Honestly, I couldn't bear to witness it, I just couldn't.

As she saw me back away, she pulled a small bundle from her purse and forced it on me. I was so worried that Grandmother would hang up that I reached for the receiver, but Maddy was too quick, and in the same fit of possessiveness she mustered the courage she needed.

"Hello?" she said.

I turned away, I'm not sure why. I heard Maddy gasp, then sob, and I knew. I had to give her her privacy. A huge weight lifted off my whole life. I'd been a camel myself for seventeen years! But no more, not after that. Especially not after what I heard next.

"It's your baby, Mama," she said.

18

Once Upon a Time

A month earlier, I would have crawled off like fresh road kill to cry my heart out, but that night damaged hearts were being resuscitated all over the world. I felt indestructible. I found Jim outside, recovering in a chair as he listened to Stefanos strum a love ballad on his passionate little bouzouki. Grandfather wanted me to sit on his lap. *Hello, I'm almost eighteen, Grandfather! I think you've had enough to drink!* I pulled up a chair beside him so he could take my hand, and he held it as he sang along. In my other hand I held the package that Maddy had forced upon me. It was a bundle of mail bound with elastic bands. Letters.

Oh, my God. The letters.

I could have spent the whole night just like that, holding those lost letters in a tight grip while soaking up Grandfather's new-found love for everything, including me. But of course I had to break the news.

"Maddy's here," I said.

I showed him the bundle of letters, which he took and turned over in his hands, flipping through them as if he knew exactly how many there were supposed to be. I took them back.

"She's over there," I said. "At Xenia's."

I helped him to his feet, which reminded me of meeting him that first day when he struggled to rise from the boat to greet me.

"She's on the phone," I said. "I think she'll be a while."

Not in my wildest dreams did I imagine that things would turn out like this, with me organizing this reunion. With me being the one who would bring this family together.

"Guess who she's speaking to," I said.

He knew, all right. One last secret we'd guarded together. He wiped his brow before heading off to Xenia's under his own steam, leaving me to follow discreetly as far as the taverna door. Maddy could not believe what was headed her way, what was happening to her. There she was, caught between her mother on the long-distance line and her father, arms wide, drawing her into an embrace.

I withdrew, retreating into the street party, gripping those impossible letters. Georgio was still singing with his father, and I waved to him from the tree in the turnaround, so he would see that I was leaving, that I was headed down the peninsula lane. At the edge of the herb fields, I waited. Looking back toward the village, I saw light streaming skyward above the rooftops, fueled by the song of the bouzouki, which now had a galloping beat. But they weren't horses' hooves—it was Georgio running.

"Look, Georgio! The moon is rising."

"Where you go?" he asked.

I kissed him, another taste of our night in the olive grove.

"My mother is here, Georgio." His eyes brightened. "She and Uncle Jim need to sort things out. They need to talk. Without me. You understand, yes?"

He nodded, and I handed him the key to my room.

"Please, Georgio, give this to Maddy. She can sleep there. They'll look for me, so please tell them I'm sleeping at Jim's tonight, okay? Jim and Danda are staying at her place."

"I come with you," he said.

"I'm fine, really. This is the happiest day of my life."

"Yes?"

"Yes."

Georgio pocketed the key. "First, I come with you," he said. "Is dark."

"Very sweet of you, but I think I know the way by now."

"No, is dangerous for you." His gaze fell on my belly. "I come and save you," he said.

"You've saved me already, Georgio. Seriously, you have no idea."

Imagine that, he wanted to save my life. Who in the history of the world had ever wanted to do that for me? And not just me, but a baby that wasn't even his.

"Okay, as far as the beach," I said, taking his hand.

Once we were over the hump of the peninsula, I stopped to listen to faint strains of music that seemed to trickle down from the heavens.

"You are staying how long in Afionas?"

"Don't know," I said, looking up at stars that studded the sky right to the horizon.

"We build a new school," he said. "Your baby will like here very much. We will like very much if you stay Afionas. Nothing to worry with Georgio."

"Thank you, Georgio."

As much as I loved him, and I did, I felt that fate probably had its own plans in store for each of us. The story of Odysseus was too much with me, how fate had sent him on a journey that lasted ten years. The gods seemed to know what they were doing, preparing him for a return to his family. I felt that fate was doing the same for me.

"You will always mean so much to me, Georgio."

We ran the last two hundred metres to the top of the escarpment, the quartzy gravel beneath my feet glowing in the moonlight, so that it was like skipping across the universe on a ribbon of moonlight. I knew then, without a doubt, that I would keep my baby. Then it was down Georgio's rope and onto that sandy little isthmus where, true to his word, he began climbing his way back up.

"Hey," he called back. "I am true. Nothing to worry with Georgio!"

• • •

Roxana's wedding tree made the perfect fire, as it cast more than enough light by which to read those letters. The splinters and twigs that lay around the courtyard provided kindling that spit and swore and crackled, then settled down into smooth-talking tongues of flame that wanted to tell more stories than I could keep track of. The cat kept me company.

In one of the letters—Maddy would have been five years old— Grandpa mentioned a friend of his named Oscar. By that time both of them had sworn off women, which, okay, I had no problem with, knowing what I know now, that love can be a shipwreck. They'd spent most of their lives in search of a safe harbour for their broken hearts, and writing about it.

Raging in the heart of the fire was a perfect storm, in which I could see their hero, Odysseus, washed ashore after his shipwreck, rolled up in his sail like a worm in a cocoon. Had Danda put that scene in my head when she described my grandfather's accident, or was it my own imagination at work? It could have been flotsam tossed up onto the deserted beach of my brain after one of my stormy dreams. Whatever it was, myth and fact had spun themselves into a single thread of memory—my grandfather waiting to be reborn.

"Grandfather in a cocoon, it's positively mythic," I say.

"Don't talk," Maddy says.

I was hoping it would distract her, since the bus is lurching and leaning more than ever.

"Keep your eye on the horizon, Maddy—it's what sailors do if they're feeling nauseous."

"What horizon?" she says.

She's right. Out the right-hand window it's a sheer wall of rock, and across the valley granite spires soar to the clouds.

"Concentrate on the apricot trees, then," I say.

I shiver at the thought of how I trashed Jim's tree. But if I hadn't, would he have been angry enough to smash that old typewriter and then break down and finally open up about Roxana Khan? That's a conversation I will never forget: me, the cat and Grandfather's broken heart. I had to coax him and crank him up like an old car engine.

"Lookin' back on it, Roxy, it was the lot of us with broken hearts."

I said nothing, just let him look back on it with the occasional glance at Oscar flickering lifelike in the light of the little candle. I sat cross-legged on the ottoman in front of Grandfather so that he'd know I wasn't going anywhere.

"Why didn't you tell her father you were married before they left?"

"Ye want to be extremely careful when it comes to a man's honour," he said. "We'd gone behind his back, acted without his permission. And now his wife was dying. We had to be very careful how we handled it."

"But you had to tell him," I said. "She was your wife."

"I had a plan. I went to see him in his hotel room. I asked him for permission to court his daughter—all old-fashioned and proper."

"What did he say?"

"Let's put it this way: he didn't take too kindly to the idea. Was I tryin' to steal her from her people? Didn't I know she had a duty to her village? Why do you think they sent her to be trained as a midwife? He worked himself up to a right fury."

"But you could have gone back to Kashmir with her, couldn't you? You could even have become Muslim, if that's what they wanted."

"Aye, and I was ready to tell him that. But not after the bomb he dropped on me next—news that Roxana herself had not yet been told—that her soldier boy had recently returned from the war."

"Her betrothed?" I asked. "He was alive?"

"For almost two years he'd been held a prisoner of war in Pakistan. Now he was back. So now, of course, he would be marryin' Roxana."

"But," I said, and then I stopped as I realized the impossible situation he'd gotten himself into. "But she was already married to you. She had a baby!"

"Well I could hardly tell him that then, could I? He was on the verge of strangling me as it was. He made it crystal clear that this chapter of her life would remain behind in Scotland. Under no circumstances could it be allowed to catch up with her. She would resume her former life as if nothin' had happened. I couldna have contact with her of any kind. And in the strongest imaginable terms, he advised me to consider her dead."

"And that's what you did," I said.

"For my own sanity," he said.

So that's why he invented the story about her dying in childbirth, I thought.

"But, Grandpa—wouldn't her betrothed be able to figure out—you know—that she wasn't a virgin anymore?"

"Aye, there's the rub," he said. "Her betrothed would reject her, ye're right. Ye've found the crux of this appalling matter."

"I think I'm going to cry," I said.

"I assure ye, nothing would be more appropriate, but before ye begin, I'll let ye in on a little secret."

"Not more secrets," I said.

"I knew what nobody else did, my dear—that her betrothed may have very well accepted her."

"How did you know that?" I asked.

"Well, when I first met your grandmother—God bless her—she was no virgin. She and her betrothed—I believe I mentioned that they loved each other very much—well, they had previously had a liaison, you see. Top secret, as ye can imagine. So the lad was not expectin' a virgin on his wedding night."

I was speechless.

"Six months later," Jim said, "I went looking for your grandmother."

"Yes!"

"Against the strong advice of the British Consul. He warned me I was asking for a heap of trouble. But I had to know what had become of her."

"And bring her back if she was unhappy," I said.

"Exactly."

"You didn't take Maddy with you," I said.

"I left her with my sister."

"So you followed Grandma to Shangri-La?"

"Now there's a road worth talkin' about. The old Silk Road from India to China. My God, Roxy, it's remote. You mention the name Hunza to a Kashmiri and he goes all misty-eyed. Nearly impossible to get in, as I found out. Bloody hell! Before we got there, half the mountain came down and wiped out the road in front of us. We were there almost two weeks clearing away the rocks and debris. Oh, aye, I could have slipped away after a few days, many did, but the strangest thing happened. One young man working by my side turned out to be Roxana's soldier boy, would ye believe?"

"I'll believe anything at this point," I said.

"The nicest young man ye've ever met. He had indeed married our Roxana. And of course he knew nothing about myself or the wee Matabhan."

Grandpa had tears in his eyes. So did I.

"I remember his name to this day," Grandfather said. "Hassan Ali."

"I guess you didn't continue on after that," I said.

We sat there in silence, both of us teary-eyed.

"When I returned to Scotland," Grandpa said, "Gretchen agreed to care for Maddy while I took a contract in Africa. Ye might be interested to know that I met a writer there, by the name of Oscar Hartmann."

"I loved Oscar," I said.

"It pleases me greatly to hear ye say that," he said. "He was like a brother. Aye, from the day I met him. My only family. Until you showed up."

• • •

Maddy is sweating.

"We're almost there, Mom."

Her bony chest is heaving, not a good sign. She's about to puke. I hurry up the aisle to ask the driver to pull over so that we can let her off the bus. Passengers offer us water and shade and kind words in some strange but musical language, and I'm sure that half of them are grateful themselves for the break.

Within minutes of planting our feet on solid ground and Maddy recovering somewhat in the fresh air, we feel a rumble in the earth. Everyone looks up in horror at the rising of a monumental roar. The driver and his assistant are the first to leap into action, wedging the wheels with stones while people take cover under the bus, as if it's a familiar drill. Maddy and I join them, face down on hot gritty asphalt where I'm sure every one of us is praying for the earth to quit shaking. After a moment, people crawl out to see what's happening. From up the road and around the next bend, a cloud of dust mushrooms out of the valley, like a nuclear explosion. We're all horror and relief, giddy with knowing we're safe. Someone embraces Maddy in gratitude, and then it's another person, and then this sudden recognition that she's their hero, because stopping has saved us from the avalanche, no doubt about it.

Traffic piles up behind us, people chattering and nattering with excitement and disappointment. Most of the vehicles head back, but not before offering lifts to bus passengers, because the bus is staying put for now.

"We're leaving, come on," Maddy says.

"Why?" I say.

"Why? Are you blind?" I'm glad to see that she's recovered. "Sweetie, if this isn't a bad sign, I don't know what is."

"It's not a sign, Mom, it's an avalanche. They happen all the time up here. You want a sign, look there."

On the back of the bus, barely visible through a coating of dust, is a tourist advertisement that says, THIS WAY TO SHANGRI-LA!

"Stop it," she says. "You've got Shangri-La on the brain."

She can mock my Shangri-La all she wants, but I'm not stopping.

I'll stay here for two weeks if I have to, like Grandfather did, digging with his bare hands to clear the road to reach Roxana. People are saying, as avalanches go, this one isn't so big, and that they'll have a footpath carved through the rubble by morning.

"Oh yes, men are working all the night," says our bus driver. "Bus on other side will be waiting. Not to worry."

We're spending the night on the bus. Perhaps I should've listened to Maddy, because I'm freezing! Most passengers have hitched rides back to the last town we passed, which is a long way back by my reckoning. But at least they're in real beds. We've put on layers of clothes, but my hands and nose are ice cubes. I must have nodded off, because my dream still lingers, the same one in which Grandmother is running from me and I try to tell her that she doesn't have to hide, it's been a mistake. In fact, we have something of hers. My recollection is kind of vague, maybe it's something she's won, and she looks at me as if I'm it. *Me?* I wake with a jolt, like I've been poked. Of course, the prize isn't me. It's Maddy.

I flinch again.

I definitely felt something—a kick? *Don't tell me, it's her.* And why not—she's about to meet her great-grandmother. If there's a special delivery on this bus, it's not Maddy or me. It's the baby.

Outside the bus, barely visible in the dim light of dawn, a medical team stands around half frozen. They pass a Thermos back and forth. Boy, I could use a cup of tea. No sign of anyone injured, which is a relief. Even the search dog has nothing to do. I curl up again and close my eyes and concentrate on my baby. Those kicks, they've totally woken me up, although I'm still exhausted and badly in need of sleep.

I hear someone step quietly into the bus. Old buses creak like crazy. The person must be standing; I think I hear them counting. There's nine of us. Tea must be on the way. *Wishful thinking!* Someone's coming up the aisle now, whispering to a passenger, such a heartwarming sound, murmurs in the night, doesn't matter what language it is. The person stops beside me now. *Ahh, a blanket.* Falling gently over my body, very nice, very nice. Better than tea. She leans over to cover my legs and I catch her sweet smoky scent. Like almonds. I open my eyes. Hers are only inches from mine, and they're not dark at all, but the colour of a clear dawn.

Oh, my God. It's her. It's Roxana.

She shushes me with a finger to her lips, and smiles. She kisses me on the forehead. I can't believe what's happening. My baby kicks. Slowly, slowly, this heavenly woman straightens up and glances at the seat behind me, then back to me with an inquiring look. I nod. From behind me, from Maddy, I can hear only deep breathing. Then I hear the rustle of a blanket being tucked around her, and the fleshy blink of another soft kiss.

My baby kicks again. She wants out, and who can blame her? It's her hungry heart, starving.

I know all about it, darling.

And I wonder, just a thought, but one that's been creeping up on me—could she have infected me with her own desire? Is that even remotely possible? Could my unborn child have led us here, Maddy and me, so that Grandmother could deliver us all at once into a brand new world?

ABOUT THE AUTHOR

Roxy *is PJ Reece's second novel for teens. PJ's first book,* Smoke That Thunders, *was published in 1999. An award-winning cinematographer and writer for television and film, PJ lives in Vancouver, but has travelled to far-flung places all over the world.*